THE
BEASTLY
ARMS

PATRICK JENNINGS

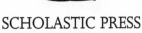

SCHOLASTIC PRESS
NEW YORK

THANKS TO

RUTH, ANNE, AND LIZ;

MATT COOK; BRIGITTE BERG;

AND ALISON, FOR LISTENING LIKE AN OWL.

LIBRARY OF CONGRESS CATALOGING-IN-PUBLICATION DATA

Jennings, Patrick.
The Beastly Arms / by Patrick Jennings.
p. cm.
Summary: Eleven-year-old Nickel, a boy with a great affinity for both animals and photography, moves into an apartment building run by the strange and mysterious Mr. Beastly and discovers a secret about the other tenants.
[1. Apartment houses — Fiction. 2. City and town life — Fiction.
3. Animals — Fiction. 4. Photography — Fiction.] I. Title.

PZ7.J4298715 Be 2001
[Fic] — dc21   00034450

ISBN 0-439-16589-X

10 9 8 7 6 5 4 3 2 1   01 02 03 04 05
Printed in the United States of America   37
First edition, May 2001

The display type was set in Ablefont.
The text type was set in 13-point Joanna.
Title page illustration by Giselle Potter
Book design by Marijka Kostiw

FOR ODETTE,
LA BÊTE MAGNIFIQUE

PART ONE

IN
THE
GARDENVIEW

1

"*WE'RE* moving," Nickel said to Miriam.

He lifted her out of her box and slipped her into his shirt pocket. She resumed nibbling the sunflower seed she'd been working on before Nickel had scooped her up. Miriam was a kangaroo rat.

"Mr. Youdle raised the rent again," Nickel said, sitting on the edge of his bed. "That's the third time in three years." He looked down into Miriam's black eyes. She laid off her nibbling. "Mom says we can't afford to live here anymore. She says we can't afford this neighborhood anymore. We may have to move downtown."

Nickel's voice was soft and frail as he said this, so Miriam tucked her seed into her cheek and hopped up his shirt front. Nickel tilted his head forward and made a puckering sound with his mouth. This was Miriam's cue to tickle his lips with her whiskers.

"We're going apartment-hunting this weekend," Nickel said in a whisper as he stroked Miriam's tiny back with the tip of his forefinger. Forgetting her legs and her long tail, she was the size and shape of a robin's egg. "She says we're going to have to cut corners around here. I'm supposed to cut down on my shooting."

Nickel stood suddenly, walked to his dresser and took his brown leather camera bag out of his top drawer. He opened it and lifted his camera out. His mother had given it to him when he was nine. Grandpa Wilde, Nickel's mom's dad, who was also a photographer, had given it to her long before. It was an old Leica rangefinder, made in the 1950s. The body and lens were made of sheet brass with a matte, nickel-plated finish. Textured black rubber made to look like leather covered the body between the top plate and the base plate. Attached to two metal loops at the top of the camera were the ends of a worn leather neck strap, which Nickel flipped over his head without thinking. It was a reflex. Miriam dodged the strap as Nickel brought the camera down against his belly. Miriam had reflexes, too.

Nickel checked the exposure counter; he'd already shot twenty-three pictures. "Better get another roll," he muttered to himself.

Miriam shuddered. She dreaded the cold blast of the refrigerator, where Nickel stored his film.

Nickel took a pack of lens tissue out from his drawer, withdrew one, removed the camera's aluminum lens cap, and gently rubbed the lens and viewfinder. It was something Miriam had seen him do a thousand times. Next came the filter. Nickel took out a rose-colored one from his camera bag and carefully screwed it onto the lens. Miriam could have bet her whiskers that next he would take out another tissue and wipe the filter — and that's exactly what he did. Then he replaced the lens cap. They were ready to go.

"I'm· going out, Mom," Nickel said as he passed through the living room.

His mom was sitting on the couch with her face in her hands. Her long black hair, with its streaks of gray, fell forward like a curtain.

Nickel stopped and set his hand on her back. Her muscles felt hard.

His mom drew her hair back and tucked it behind her ear. "Going shooting?" she asked, trying to smile.

Nickel nodded and tried to smile back.

"What filter?" his mom asked, looking down at the camera around Nickel's neck.

"A red."

"I know what *that* means," his mom said, this time really smiling. "Try to be back by six. I have to be at work at seven."

"Okay," Nickel said, but he didn't get up to go.

"Well, what are you waiting for?" his mom asked. "You don't have much time. The golden hour is upon us!"

Nickel liked it when she said that. The golden hour was when the light outside was best, when it was warm and soft and honeyed. Photographers love the golden hour — photographers like Nickel and his mom.

"Want to come with?" Nickel asked.

His mom leaned forward and kissed him on the forehead. "No. I need to make dinner. You go ahead. Have fun. Make me a picture." Her eyes glistened.

Nickel gave her a kiss good-bye, then he and Miriam went out the door into the hall. They were down all three flights of stairs and out onto the street before Miriam realized that Nickel had forgotten all about the refrigerator — and the film. His absentmindedness paid off sometimes.

Ira Monk Street, where Nickel and his mom lived, was jammed with honking cars and growling trucks. Instead of golden light, Nickel saw brown smutch. He covered his mouth and nose with his sleeve and ran to the corner, turning right onto 17th Street. It was choked with traffic and smog as well. At this time of year, the golden hour was also rush hour.

Nickel ran down 17th, holding his camera away from his body to keep it from banging against him. At Hill Avenue, he turned left. His thigh muscles tightened as the sidewalk steepened. He crossed 18th, then 19th. At 20th, he was wheezing. At 21st, he was pumping his thighs with his hands, helping them as they worked. At 22nd, he was panting. At 23rd was Flood Hill Park.

He passed between adults circling the park with their dogs and by adults on benches watching their children playing on the playground. He ran up the concrete stairway that started wide at the bottom and gradually grew narrower as it went up. At the top of the stairs, he kept right on going — up the grassy slope, through the orderly clumps of trees, up to the summit.

Then, high above the snarling, boxy city below — it reminded Nickel of a zoo — he stretched out on his back on the grass and gazed up at the sky. It was magenta with streaks of gold. The clouds glowed amber, like the yield light on a traffic signal. Nickel lay there, huffing and puffing, his camera riding up and down on his belly, waiting for his chest to stop heaving and his breath to resume its normal, silent rhythm. When it did, he brought his camera up to his eye, popped off the lens cap, pulled out the collapsible lens, and aimed it upward.

Most photographers use a light meter to determine the proper settings for exposure, but Nickel didn't own one, and he didn't need one. He'd been shooting the same subject for so long that he could gauge how much light there was just by looking at it. Usually he set the aperture at f8 — about half open — and set the shutter speed to one five-hundredth of a second, which was fast. Sometimes he had to adjust these settings if the sky was particularly bright or unusually dark. However, he always set the focus to ∞ — to infinity. This ensured that all subjects seventeen feet or more away from the lens would be in focus. His subjects were always in focus. They were always more than seventeen feet away.

Nickel shot clouds.

"It's a sea cow," he said to Miriam, who had crept out of his pocket and was searching the grass for seeds and nuts. Nickel pressed the shutter release. The camera clicked. The sea cow became the twenty-third exposure on his roll. He twisted the film advance with his finger and thumb. The exposure counter now read 24. He tilted the camera slightly. "There's a kangaroo lying on its back," he said. Click. He advanced the film, tilted the camera again. "There's a musk-ox." Click. Advance. Tilt. "There's a mud puppy, catching a ball." Click. Advance. Tilt. "And the shrew who threw it!" Click. Advance. Tilt. "There's a barn owl, swooping." Click. Advance. Tilt. He went on like this until, while aiming at a potato beetle munching a potato leaf, he pressed the shutter and it wouldn't give.

He sat up. "Out of film," he muttered to himself. He patted his pants pockets for his backup roll. There was no backup roll.

"Did I forget to stop for film?" he asked Miriam.

She didn't answer.

"I guess I did," Nickel said to himself, shaking his head.

He set his camera down in the grass and looked out at the city. Lights were coming on in the windows. Headlights and streetlights were coming on, too. The clouds were now mottled red and gold. The smog between them and the city was brown and heavy. The evening breeze was beginning to blow it out to the suburbs. The sun was gone.

Nickel closed one eye and covered his building — Mr. Youdle's building, the Gardenview Apartments — with the tip of his forefinger. All seven floors of it disappeared. It was that simple. One second, his building was there. The next, it wasn't.

Good-bye, Gardenview Apartments, Nickel thought with a sigh.

2

ZINDEL'S produce market was mobbed when Nickel walked by on the way home. Men and women wearing suits and carrying plastic bags and briefcases sniffed melons, weighed onions, and squeezed tomatoes. Mrs. Zindel waved at Nickel as he passed. She always reminded him of a white-browed gibbon, with her pale eyes and bushy gray eyebrows. But he never told her so.

For reasons Nickel never understood, people didn't like being compared to primates. Nickel enjoyed comparing himself to them. After all, he was one. He liked looking at his reflection in the mirror and noting how his features resembled those of a bush baby. He had the same oversized eyes, the same pointy snout, the same perky ears. Because of this, the kids at school sometimes teased him, but they never did so accurately. They called him Owl Boy or Dumbo, but he didn't look at all like an owl or an elephant. He looked like a bush baby, the little furry primate with fingers and a tail that lives in trees and can see in the dark. Only Inez said he looked like one, but that was only because he'd told her how he felt about it. Inez was his best friend.

Sixto's newsstand was doing the same brisk business as Zindel's market. The men and women in suits picked out their own papers and magazines and handed Sixto the money. He never said a word to any of them. Sixto had big black circles around his eyes and was wearing a white vest over a black shirt. He was a panda.

Mr. Huddleston, the flower-stand man, was a bobcat, with his goatee and hairy ears, and Agatha, the pie lady, was a walrus. She sold her homemade pies on the corner of 17th and Ivy for three dollars apiece every evening at six.

Nickel looked down at Miriam in his pocket.

"We're late," he said.

He hurried ahead into the street against the light. Tires squealed and a horn blared. Nickel covered his ears and ran for the curb, his camera bouncing against his stomach. He turned left a block later onto Ira Monk Street and sprinted the last half black to his building. At the Gardenview, he pressed number 317 (he'd forgotten his key) and waited. He shifted his weight from one foot to the other, as if he were still running.

"Forget your key?" his mom's voice crackled over the intercom.

Nickel couldn't tell if she was angry. "Uh-huh," he answered.

"Well, hurry on up," the intercom said. "Your dad wants to talk to you."

The door buzzed and Nickel pushed it open.

"Late *and* Dad," he said to his reflection in the mirrored tiles in the foyer. "I'm dead."

He plodded up the stairs to his apartment, imagining his dad standing in the doorway, wearing a gray suit, a blue shirt, a green tie. His face would be red, his lips, white. His thinning auburn hair would be combed forward to hide his bald spot. Nickel's dad was an orangutan — an orangutan in a gray suit. To Nickel, of course, this wasn't necessarily a bad thing.

When he reached his apartment, he found his dad wasn't there. His mom was inside, standing in their tiny kitchen, the cordless phone tucked under her chin. She was wearing her comfortable shoes and her apron with the pad and pen in the pocket. She was dressed for her night job at Delphinium, where she waited tables.

"He's *eleven!*" she was saying into the phone. She was angry. "And this is *his* neighborhood! People around here know him! They look out for him!"

"I saw Agatha selling her pies." Nickel said meekly. "I didn't know it was already six."

His mom peeked over at him and smiled. "It's all right," she said, covering the mouthpiece with her hand. Her anger dimmed. "Come eat your dinner."

Nickel sat at the table that, as always, was pushed into the corner under the small kitchen window. The window looked out onto the kitchen windows of some of the building's other apartments. He saw Ms. Coats putting on a kettle, and Ms. McPhee washing dishes. Mr. Ojeda was eating alone. Nickel set his camera down then took a bite of his dinner — leftover ratatouille from Delphinium. He broke off a bit of a cracker and dropped it into his pocket for Miriam.

"I'm not going to move out to the suburbs!" Nickel's mom snapped into the phone. Her anger flared again, and she stormed off toward her room. "Next thing you'll be wanting me to buy a *car!*" she said. Nickel heard her door slam.

Nickel's mom and dad were always having this argument. His dad wanted them to move out to Oak Hollow — which was about forty miles from downtown and where he and his new wife, Julie, lived — or at least out of the city. He didn't think the city was a good place for Nickel to grow up. Nickel's mom wanted him to butt out.

The door to her room reopened a few minutes later. "Look," she said as she strode back into the kitchen, "either we find a place in town or we'll head out to the country. It's either city life or wildlife. I certainly don't want a *dead* life."

She applied dark red lipstick to her bottom lip with a quick flick of her wrist, then pressed both lips together. She'd put eye makeup on in her room. Nickel knew she didn't like wearing it. When she wore it she looked sad. Instead of a lemur — which is what she looked most like to Nickel — she looked more like a sloth.

"Listen, Nick, how would it be if you ran your life, and I ran mine?" she said.

Nickel had been named for his dad. They were both Nicholas Dill. But neither was ever called Nicholas, except in formal situations, like in divorce court or on the first day of school. Nickel's mom started the "Nickel" thing when he was a baby. To him, it was just a name. It was the kids at school that couldn't seem to forget it was also a five-cent coin. (Buffalo Head was another of their favorite nicknames for him.)

He looked back out the window. The open space between all the kitchens began at the ground, in a kind of courtyard. It was a bare, six-sided slab of cement. No plants, no earth. Still, it was the only thing resembling a garden anywhere in the vicinity of the Gardenview Apartments. The hexagonal space it created between the kitchens of the building rose up seven floors to a hexagonal view of the sky, which was now dark. Blue-gray clouds drifted across the purple sky. Nickel saw a blue-gray octopus, its tentacles trailing behind it. Then a blue-gray Galápagos turtle. Then a blue-gray flea.

"Your dad wants to speak to you," his mom said to Nickel, startling him.

When he turned around she was holding the phone out to him. He took it and said, "Hi, Dad."

"Can't you talk some sense into her?" his dad said. He sounded exasperated. "You want to move out here, don't you?"

Nickel thought of Oak Hollow, with its curved, wide streets and its short buildings. Instead of parking meters on the curbs, there were mailboxes. There were no news-stands or produce markets or pie ladies. There were malls and convenience stores and parking lots and empty side-walks. Nickel hardly ever saw anyone that wasn't in a car.

He liked where he lived better.

"Well, look, son," his dad said without waiting for Nickel's reply. "See what you can do. Make her see reason."

Nickel didn't really understand what his dad was asking him, but he answered, "Okay." He'd learned that that was the answer his dad usually wanted.

"Good man," his dad said. "Now, I don't want to hear again that you're out traipsing around the city at night. It's not safe."

"Okay," Nickel said again.

"Don't you have homework?"

"Uh-huh," Nickel said.

"What is it?"

"Rational numbers."

"Well, see, I could help you there," his dad said proudly. "Math's my specialty, you know."

Nickel's dad was an engineer. Not the train kind — the kind that sits behind a desk.

"I know," Nickel said.

"But I can't help you way out here. Maybe if you lived closer." He paused for effect. "You work on your mom."

"Okay," Nickel said.

"Good man. Now put her back on. And get at that math."

✶   ✶   ✶

"Can I come to the darkroom tomorrow after school?" Nickel asked his mom after she'd gotten off the phone. His mom taught photography at City College. "I have film to develop."

"Sure," his mom answered. She sat down at the table beside him. "Did you take one for me?"

Nickel nodded. "A kangaroo lying on its back. You like kangaroos."

His mom smiled. "Is it good?" she asked, pointing at Nickel's bowl.

"My compliments to Dierdre," he said. Dierdre was the chef at Delphinium.

"I'll be sure to tell her," his mom said, standing up. She leaned over and kissed Nickel on the forehead, leaving two dark red lip prints. Then she left.

Nickel went to his room after dinner to do his home-work. Before he began, though, he rewound the roll in his camera and took it out. Then he put it and the camera in his drawer with the other three rolls of film he'd already exposed. He scooped Miriam out of his pocket (she was asleep) and set her down in the cardboard box he'd fashioned into a nest.

"I need to remember to get more film," he said to himself as he carried his math book to his bed. He lay on his back and looked up at the clouds. His ceiling was plastered with his photographs.

"A camel sitting on a dune," he whispered to himself. "A hare in a hat. An otter hiding its eyes . . ."

Soon he fell asleep.

3

NICKEL arrived at school the next morning just as the five-minute bell rang. It had been one of those mornings when he and his mom just couldn't seem to get out of the house. He walked as fast as he was allowed to down the hall to his classroom, and then hurried down the aisle to his desk. He sat down seconds before the final bell. Mr. Kirkaby smiled at him from the front of the room.

"Just in time, Mr. Dill," he said.

Mr. Kirkaby always called his students by their last names, preceded by either Mr. or Ms. Most of the students didn't mind. Finbar Quinn preferred it, in fact. But some didn't like it at all. Heather Spitzenheimer, for example. And Scott Pfister — Mister Pfister. Nickel wasn't fond of it, either. Mr. Dill lent itself too easily to pickle jokes. He often wished he had been given his mom's last name instead. "Good morning, Mr. Wilde," Mr. Kirkaby would say. Nickel liked the sound of that.

As always, Mr. Kirkaby took roll from his seat, then the class listened to Ms. Stonecipher, the principal, read the morning announcements over the intercom. She reminded everyone that there would be no class on Monday due to parent–teacher conferences. Nickel had forgotten all about that. He hoped his mom hadn't. He hadn't even told his dad about it. His dad could never get away for such things. The only time he actually agreed to attend one, he called Mr. Kirkaby at the last minute and canceled.

After the announcements, Mr. Kirkaby stood before the class and said what he said every morning since the school year began.

"Another day on Earth. Let's make the most of it."

Making the most of it that morning meant going over the math homework. Nickel hadn't done his, so he spent most of this time watching a small triangle of light, which was reflecting off Mr. Kirkaby's chrome-plated stapler, crawl up the blackboard in a diagonal path toward the clock. It was yellow-colored as the day began but became whiter and whiter as the morning progressed. When Mr. Kirkaby excused the class for recess, Nickel remained in his seat, transfixed by the triangle and his thoughts of moving from the Gardenview Apartments.

"Mr. Dill?" Mr. Kirkaby said. "Aren't you going out?"

Nickel didn't hear him. He wasn't hearing right then.

Mr. Kirkaby stepped in front of Nickel's desk, breaking his line of vision. The triangle disappeared. Nickel looked up, confused.

"Did you get enough sleep last night, Mr. Dill?" Mr. Kirkaby asked.

Nickel nodded vaguely.

"Are you feeling all right?"

Nickel nodded vaguely again.

"Cat got your tongue?" Mr. Kirkaby said with a grin.

Cat? Nickel thought, moving his tongue around inside his mouth. He hadn't used it all morning and it felt groggy.

"I noticed you didn't have your homework," Mr. Kirkaby said. He knelt down in front of Nickel's desk. His eyes were deep-set and pale brown. The skin around them was dark. He had short, bristly, silvery hair and a sharp nose and rather large ears. He was a gray fox.

"I didn't do it," Nickel said softly.

"Well, it's good to hear your voice at least!" Mr. Kirkaby said, smiling.

Nickel smiled a little, too.

"Didn't you understand it?" Mr. Kirkaby asked.

"I didn't even look at it," Nickel said. "I fell asleep."

Mr. Kirkaby nodded. "Well, don't worry about it. Why don't you just turn it in on Tuesday?" He rose to his feet. His knees cracked. "Maybe you ought to go out now and get some fresh air. It'll do you a world of good."

"Okay," Nickel said. He got up from his desk and started down the aisle to the door. His feet felt heavy and tingly, so he stomped as he went along.

When he pushed the door to the playground open, the light reflecting off the asphalt shined in his eyes. He shielded them with his hand.

"Nickel!" a voice called out.

Nickel peeked out from under his hand to see a silhouetted form running across the playground toward him. He couldn't see the form's face but he could tell by its gait and its gangly limbs that it was Inez. She and Nickel had been classmates in first, second, third, and fifth grades, but not in fourth or sixth. Still, they always hung out together at recess, sat together at lunch, and did things together after school and on weekends. Having a girl for a best friend didn't exactly win him points with the guys in class, but Nickel didn't care. The ones who gave him a hard time about it — like Finbar Quinn and Henry Kang — were the same guys who called him Owl Boy and Buffalo Head. They never knew what they were talking about. Nickel was much better off having Inez on his side than them. She always told them exactly where they could get off.

Inez ran up the stairs and stood so she blocked out the sun. Then she reached up and lowered Nickel's arm.

"Did you space out in class again, Mr. Dill?"

Nickel squinted at her. She was grinning ear to ear. Her black hair was braided tightly into thin rows and then bound in the back by an elastic band. Each row had a different colored ribbon tied at the end. Her brown eyes and brown skin looked creamy in the sun, like the crème caramel at Delphinium. She had a mouth filled with big, bright teeth. Inez was a spider monkey. Nickel once told her so, and she didn't mind one bit. She said she liked monkeys.

"Mom says we have to move," Nickel said.

Inez's smile drooped a little at the edges. "Where?" she asked.

"I don't know. Out of the neighborhood. She says we can't afford it anymore. Mr. Youdle raised the rent again. We may have to move downtown."

Inez sat down on the step. Nickel sat beside her. They watched the other sixth graders on the playground. A group of girls were jumping rope and chanting. Other kids swung on swings, played dodgeball, tetherball, hop-scotch, and four-square. Some of them just ran around, chasing each other, grabbing each other's things and running off with them.

"Will you still go to school here?" Inez asked, still looking out at the playground.

Nickel shrugged. "I guess it depends on where we end up."

Inez suddenly grinned. "Well, don't worry about it, bush baby!" she said, punching his arm. "Maybe you won't move at all! Parents are always saying things like that. 'I guess we'll have to move!' 'I guess we won't be eating for a while!' They don't mean it. Maybe your dad will help out, give her money. He's sure got enough." She rolled her eyes.

"Maybe," Nickel said. He couldn't imagine his dad offering to help — not unless his mom agreed to move out of town. And she would never do that. At least Nickel didn't think she would.

"Just forget about it, is what I say," Inez said. "Come on." She stood up. "What you need is a little exercise." She ran down the stairs.

Nickel rose slowly to his feet.

"Come on!" Inez called over her shoulder. She was making her way across the playground to the monkey bars.

Nickel stepped shakily down the stairs. When he hit the asphalt, his feet began to feel lighter and the tingling faded. He began to run. A warmth rose in his cheeks and in his chest. He ran faster, dodging kids that crossed his path. When he reached the monkey bars his momentum carried him right up to the top. He sat next to Inez, panting and laughing.

"See?" Inez said.

"For your next writing assignment," Mr. Kirkaby said ten minutes before the dismissal bell that afternoon, "I want you to conduct another interview."

He looked around at the students, gauging their reactions. Most of them grimaced. A few of them grumbled. "Oh-ooh!" Jason Gomez groaned.

"I want you to interview an adult again," Mr. Kirkaby went on. "But this time, not one of your parents, or your guardians. No one related to you. No family."

The grumbling stopped. The grimaces turned to blank stares.

"No family?" Henry Kang gasped.

"The person can't be living with you," Mr. Kirkaby went on, "and can't work here at school."

There wasn't a sound as the students searched their brains for someone who fit these restrictions. Nickel had no trouble thinking of candidates. There were the 17th Street vendors: Sixto, Mrs. Zindel, Mr. Huddleston, and Agatha the pie lady. There was also Ms. Coats and Ms.

McPhee and Mr. Ojeda in his building. Mr. Youdle crossed his mind but Nickel quickly chased the image away.

"The school newspaper will publish the interviews it finds most interesting and well-written," Mr. Kirkaby said. "But I don't want you to think too much about that. I want you to focus for the moment on who you'd like to interview. I want you to think of all the adults that you know, outside your family, outside your home, outside school. I want you to think about them carefully. Think about what you know about them. Think about what you don't know about them. Think about what you'd like to know about them. Take your time. Your homework for the three-day weekend is to think. Just to think. Then, when you finish thinking, choose. Be careful to do it in that order." He smiled. "All you need for Tuesday is a name, a carefully chosen name. Any questions?"

Scott Pfister's hand shot into the air. Scott's hand always shot into the air.

"Mr. Pfister?" Mr. Kirkaby said. Some of the children snickered at the rhyme.

"How about Billy?" Scott asked.

"Who's Billy?" Mr. Kirkaby asked back.

"He's a friend of my dad's."

"Does he live with you?"

"He lives in Idaho."

"How are you going to interview him if he lives in Idaho?"

Scott thought about this.

"*That's* it, Mr. Pfister," Mr. Kirkaby said. "Now you're doing your homework. Any other questions?" he asked the class.

No hands went up.

"Then I'll see you on Tuesday," he said. "Make the most of your long weekend."

Class was dismissed even though the last bell hadn't rung. Mr. Kirkaby always said that the school day was done when it was done and that it had nothing to do with clocks or bells. The students were not allowed out of the room, of course. Not until the bell rang.

Nickel packed up his stuff and walked over to the window. He looked up at the sky and saw two puffins dancing.

Puffins made him think of Julie, his dad's wife: She looked like one. Julie wasn't a relative (not a blood relative, anyway) and she didn't live with him and she didn't work at the school. She worked downtown in an office. Nickel didn't see her very often, though — only one Sunday a month and three weeks in August. She'd be hard to interview.

"Who are you going to interview?" a voice behind him asked. It was Scott Pfister's voice.

Nickel didn't turn around. He knew what Scott looked like. He looked like a ferret.

"I don't know," Nickel said. "I have to think about it."

4

INEZ was waiting for Nickel on the school's front steps.

"Are you going straight home?" she asked.

Sometimes Nickel went to City College after school to work in the darkroom or to the public library to check out books about animals. But if he went straight home, he and Inez walked together. She lived on 18th and Jacquet, between the school and Nickel's house.

"Uh-huh," Nickel said. "I'm going to the darkroom, but I have to pick up something at home first."

"Does this something have a long tail and whiskers?" Inez asked with a grin.

Nickel didn't need to answer.

"Do you have weekend homework?" Inez asked as they walked.

"Sort of," Nickel said. "I have to think of someone to interview."

"Me, too," Inez said. "Ms. Cardenal said we couldn't interview anyone in our family or anyone we live with or anyone at school."

"So did Mr. Kirkaby."

"I'm going to interview Mrs. Bislimi on the fifth floor," Inez said. "She moved here a few months ago from Albania. She's eighty, and has seen it all."

Nickel marveled at how confident Inez was, with her chin up and her eyes sparkling and her mind already made up. Her interview of Mrs. Bislimi would not only be selected for the school paper, it would be the best one in it. Nickel, on the other hand, would need every second of the three days to think of someone to interview, and he knew he would probably squander them thinking of a million other things.

"Would you take a picture of Mrs. Bislimi for me?" Inez asked. "It'd be so great to run a picture of her with the story."

She is already assuming her interview will be published, Nickel thought.

"Well?" she pressed. "Will you?"

Nickel's shoulders pinched up. He never liked being asked to take pictures. He only liked taking his own.

And Inez knew it.

She jabbed him with her elbow. "Sheesh!" she said, laughing. "Like I'd really even ask! You're so serious all the time!"

Nickel laughed without opening his mouth. It came out his nose, as a snort.

"So what are you doing today? Developing or printing?" she asked.

"Developing," Nickel said.

Nickel developed and printed his own pictures. His mom said it was too expensive to take them somewhere to have them done. Nickel didn't mind at all. He liked watching the pictures emerge from white paper, like magic. He liked doing it himself.

"I wonder what you shot," Inez said, elbowing him again. She threw her head back and laughed out loud.

She was teasing him again, but it was a different kind of teasing than Finbar's and Henry's. It was the kind that came from understanding.

When they reached her building, Inez suggested they go to the library on Saturday. There was going to be a program of nature films at two o'clock. Nickel said he wasn't sure he could go.

"I might be apartment-hunting with my mom," he said glumly.

"I'm telling you," Inez said, "your mom will change her mind." She walked up her steps to the front door and took out her key.

"I *want* to go with you," Nickel said.

"I know." She unlocked the door. "Call me."

She went inside and Nickel watched her through the glass door as she ran up the stairs. Inez lived on the eighth floor but always took the steps, even though her building had an elevator. She loved to climb. She often said that she would climb Mount Everest one day, all by herself, without any help. Nickel believed her.

Mr. Youdle was coming out of the Gardenview Apartments' front door as Nickel approached. He had half a sub sandwich in his hand. Instead of holding the door open for Nickel, Mr. Youdle let it shut behind him.

"Don't you have your key?" he asked, squinting down at Nickel.

Nickel dug his keys out of his pocket, then held his building key up for Mr. Youdle to see.

"Never hold the door open for anyone," Mr. Youdle said, wagging his finger. "You understand?"

Nickel nodded.

Mr. Youdle took a large bite of his sandwich. "Good!" he said with his mouth full, then he waddled off down the sidewalk.

Nickel's mom always said Mr. Youdle was a snake, but Nickel disagreed. A snake only eats when its hungry, sometimes going months without a meal. Mr. Youdle was always eating. He was a hippopotamus.

Nickel unlocked the door and raced up the stairs to his apartment. He unlocked the front door with his apartment key, then ran to his room.

"We're going to the darkroom," he said to Miriam and scooped her out of her box. She hopped up his arm to his shoulder.

Nickel put the four rolls of film from his drawer into

his pack, then carried it and Miriam into the kitchen. Miriam scurried around behind his neck in case he opened the fridge, but he just took a pear from the fruit bowl on the counter and bit into it. Then he went out the door, locked it, and ran down the stairs to the front door.

Ms. McPhee was outside it, fumbling around inside her purse, her arms filled with groceries. Nickel pulled the door open for her.

"Hello," he said, holding the door.

"Oh, thank you, young man!" she said. "I can't imagine where my keys are!"

Nickel nodded and stepped by her out into the street.

As he made his way toward the subway station, he looked up at the narrow strip of sky between the tops of the building. He often did this and many times it resulted in his bashing into or tripping over something or someone — a fireplug, say, or a newspaper dispenser. Miriam did her best to help out. If she saw trouble ahead she'd dig her claws into his chest through his shirt. That would get his attention — though not always in time.

"One day you'll walk in front of a bus and that'll be

that," his mom often scolded him. "You can't live in the clouds and in the city at the same time."

This time, he made it to the station stumbling only twice — over an orange safety cone and into a Great Dane. He descended the stairs, avoiding the sticky spills and the people sleeping there, dropped his pear stem into a trash can, and made his way to the ticket booth. He waved his transit pass at the agent. It was Vera. Vera, the woodchuck.

"Hi, Nickel," she said. "Hi, Miriam."

Nickel waved and then, hearing a train approaching below, slid down the handrail to the platform. It was a green line train. The green line went by the college. Nickel jumped aboard and he and Miriam rode underground — like moles — to where his mom taught.

His mom was sitting at her desk in her office looking through a magnifier at plastic sleeves filled with negatives when he arrived.

"Why don't you just get started?" she said without looking up. "I have a stack of these to go through."

"Okay," Nickel said and headed off down the hall to the equipment cage. As always, the smell of chemicals in the air made him wince.

"Hi, Nickel," Gwendolyn said from inside the cage. She leaned forward onto her elbows on the counter. "And hello, Miriam, hiding in Nickel's pocket." Gwendolyn was tall and lanky with freckles all over her arms and face and neck. She was a cheetah. "What are you two up to today?" she asked.

"Developing," he said.

"How many rolls?"

"Four."

Gwendolyn got out two black plastic developing tanks, four white plastic reels, and a clear plastic thermometer and slid it all across the counter to Nickel on an orange plastic tray. Then she handed him the key to Room C.

"Thanks," Nickel said.

He let himself into the darkroom and switched on the light. The room was small and cramped and spotless. Nickel put the tray down on the stainless steel counter, then dug his rolls of film out of his backpack. He arranged everything on the tray so that he could find it all in the dark, then shut out the light.

Except for the pulsating star of light left on his retina by the lightbulb, he couldn't see a thing. When he looked left, the star moved left across the blackness. When he looked right, it moved right. He closed his eyes. Nothing changed. He couldn't even see his eyelids as they slid up and down.

Miriam began to stir in his pocket. She thought night had fallen. She hopped up his shirt front to his shoulder.

"I wish I had your eyes," Nickel whispered to her.

He groped around on the counter for one of the film magazines. He always bought film in big, hundred-foot rolls and bulk-loaded it — in the dark — into magazines. The magazines were small, light-tight aluminum canisters much like the kind they sell individually in stores, except that they could be reloaded. Loading his own magazines was time-consuming, but it saved his mom money.

He slid the magazine open and gently lifted the coil of film out, careful to touch it only by its edges. He felt around with his other hand for one of the reels. When he found one, he inserted the end of the film into it. The reel was a plastic spool that held the film without allowing it to come into contact with itself. Nickel carefully inched the film onto the reel until the entire roll had been loaded, then he found one of the tanks, opened its lid, and dropped the reel inside. One down, three to go. He found another magazine and went through the whole process again. When the second loaded reel was in the tank, he replaced the lid. Then he opened the two remaining magazines, loaded them onto the other two remaining reels, set them both into the second tank, and closed its lid. Then, at last, he could breathe again.

He reached for the light switch. His hand went directly to it. He had been in the dark in Room C many times before. When the light came on, Miriam dove back into his pocket.

Nickel went to the sink and mixed up the developer — or "soup," as photographers call it. When he could, he held his nose. He checked the temperature with a thermometer and consulted a chart hung on the wall. Development would take eight minutes. Nickel set the timer and poured the soup into the tanks. He tapped them on the table to get out any air bubbles, then, one in each hand, flipped them upside down, then right side up again, then upside down, then right side up. He did this every thirty seconds until the development was done. When the timer dinged, he poured the soup out and poured in stop bath (to stop the action of any developer still left inside). After thirty seconds, he poured the stop bath out and poured in the fix, which makes the negatives permanent. When the fixing was complete, he opened the tanks. He inserted two rubber hoses into the center of the reels and turned on the water. The film had to be washed for five minutes. Then he could see what he had.

His heart always froze upon unwinding the first roll of film. He always worried that something had gone wrong, that the film would be clear, or fogged, or black, or that he had rolled it badly and it had fused together. But this time, like most times, everything was fine. No fog, no fusing, just a row of negative images with the normal assortment of different grays. Nickel attached a hanging clip to the end of the strip and hung it from a line over the sink, then attached a weighted clip to the bottom to keep it from curling. Now he could look more closely at the individual pictures. He tilted his head sideways. In each little rectangle on the strip he saw a dark gray cloud surrounded by lighter gray.

He unwound and hung the other rolls — they were fine, too — then moved them to the film-drying cabinet, where he swabbed them with photowipes. Then he flipped the sign on the cabinet door from EMPTY to DO NOT DISTURB, and washed up, tidied up, and locked up the room.

"Finished?" Gwendolyn asked as he handed in his equipment.

Nickel nodded.

"So, what are you working on?" Gwendolyn asked, with a knowing grin.

"Some pictures," Nickel said.

Gwendolyn laughed. "I wonder what of!"

Nickel's mom was still looking at negatives when Nickel returned.

"How'd they come out?" she asked, looking up.

"Fine," Nickel said, sitting in a chair.

"Are you hungry?"

"I had a pear."

"Well, I'm starved. I brought the rest of the ratatouille and some cheese sandwiches. How does that sound?"

"Okay," Nickel said.

"Just let me finish these up," his mom said. "Do you have homework?"

"Sort of. I can't do it here."

"Well, I'll just be a minute." She lifted a sheet of negatives and began examining it. "These guys are pretty good. Best beginners I've had in years."

"Mom," Nickel said, staring at his shoes. "Do we really have to move?"

His mom set down the negatives and sighed. She raised her hand to her mouth and pinched her lips with her fingers. She often did this before saying something she didn't like to say.

"I'm afraid so," she said. "I'd like to start looking tomorrow morning. Will you come with me?"

Nickel's shoulders slumped. "Inez wants me to go to the library with her," he muttered.

"I'd like you to come with me. We'll be looking for a place for both of us, you know."

Nickel rubbed his nose with his knuckle, then winced. It smelled like fix.

"Okay," he said.

5

NICKEL'S mom was drinking coffee and drawing red circles in the classified section the next morning when Nickel came into the kitchen.

"Slim pickings," she said without looking up.

"Did you eat?" Nickel asked.

"Some toast."

Nickel opened the fridge before Miriam could prepare herself and the cold blast shot deep into her tiny bones. Nickel could feel her shivering.

"Sorry," he said.

He took out a jar of lemon curd, sliced off a slab of bread from the loaf on the cutting board, and sat down next to his mother. Ms. Coats was across the courtyard, sitting at her kitchen table, sipping from a coffee cup.

"Did you call Inez last night?" his mom asked.

"Uh-huh," Nickel said, spreading the lemon curd onto his bread. "I'm going to meet her at the library if we finish in time. The program's at two."

"It's possible," his mom said. "I can't imagine any of these will be worth seeing, considering where they are. Naturally, the only places we can afford are in the worst neighborhoods. The trick of finding a nice affordable apartment in this city is to stay put. Every time you move you end up with a worse place for the same money. Of course, you have to stay put in a place that isn't run by a snake." She looked up and sighed. "We may have to stay here anyway."

Nickel hid a smile. He didn't want his mom to know how much he wanted to stay. It wasn't that he liked the Gardenview so much. He just didn't want to leave the neighborhood. Still, he didn't want his mom to base her decision on him. In his opinion, she was the better decision-maker of the two.

"Maybe we should move out to the country," his mom said. "Live in a cabin in the woods, like Laura Ingalls Wilder, or Henry David Thoreau. Why do all these rugged, outdoorsy types have three names?"

Nickel could tell she wasn't being serious. She sometimes talked like this — about moving out into the wilderness, hewing a living off the land, breathing fresh air, and eating food right out of the ground. But it would pass.

"No," his mom said, "I guess we couldn't do that, could we? That would take money — money and a country job. What could I do in the country? What do I know about country living, about farming, about living off the land?"

"We could raise animals," Nickel said.

"What do I know about raising animals?"

"I know about animals."

His mom smiled. "Yes, you do. You know a lot about animals. But animals aren't free, you know. They don't grow on trees."

"Birds do," Nickel said.

"Okay, okay," his mom said. "Let's keep this thing in focus. We can't leave the city. We can't afford to. And we can't afford it here anymore. Even if we could, what's to stop Youdle from raising the rent *again* in six months?"

She sighed and folded her newspaper. "Finish eating and we'll go," she said.

☼   ☼   ☼

Nickel's mom had guessed right: None of the apartments for rent in their price range were worth looking at. She could tell just from the buildings they were in. One by one, she crossed out her red circles.

"Maybe I need to lower my standards," she said as they headed yet farther downtown. "The one over on 6th wasn't so bad."

"You mean the one over the liquor store?" Nickel asked.

His mom groaned. "Never mind," she said.

It was nearly noon when she scratched off the last circle.

"Are you hungry?" she asked.

Nickel nodded.

"There's a little Mediterranean café around here." She looked around. "I think it's over on 2nd. Let's cut through here."

She pointed at the entrance to an alley up ahead. As they neared it, Nickel looked for a street sign, but couldn't find one. The alley was so narrow and the buildings so high that, though it was midday, the light was dusky.

"Oh, it doesn't go through!" his mom said suddenly. Her voice sounded hollow, like she was speaking into a empty can.

There was a wall at the end of the alley with a door in it — a drab, gray, windowless door. On it, Nickel spied a small, shiny brass plate. It was reflecting a golden rectangle of light on the ground.

Nickel's mom turned around and started walking back toward the street. "Come on," she said, exasperated.

"Wait!" Nickel said. His voice echoed.

His mom stopped in her tracks. She looked back with a cross expression. "What?" she said.

Nickel didn't answer. He just kept walking toward the door, toward the brass plate.

"What are you doing?" his mom snapped. "Where are you going?"

Nickel couldn't hear her. He was lost in the soft light, mesmerized by the reflection of the brass plate.

"Oh, for —!" his mom said, and began walking briskly after him.

As Nickel reached the door, he tripped over the shallow doorstep — he was walking without looking down — and fell forward. Miriam scrambled out of his pocket and scurried up the back of his neck into his hair. Nickel put his hands out to brace himself and his left one fell against the doorbell. His head banged against the door. He heard chiming and saw stars.

"Nickel!" his mom said, running up the alley. "Are you all right?"

As she helped him to his feet, Nickel's eyes focused on the brass plate. It read:

The Beastly Arms Apartments

"Did you hurt your —" his mom began to say when the clicking of a lock silenced her. The gray door began to open. She and Nickel both watched in silence as the dark crack grew slowly wider and wider, until the door was standing fully open. Whoever had opened it did not appear.

"We're sorry," Nickel's mom said in a shaky voice. "We didn't mean to knock. My son tripped and —"

Her voice broke off as an ear appeared at the door's edge. Nickel thought that it looked like a seashell. A face followed. It was a man's face, a wrinkled face, a tired face. A very tired face. It looked as if it had just been roused from a ten-year nap. On the man's head was wispy white hair, like an infant's; on his chin, a wiry, salt-and-pepper beard. His eyes were big and dark, like Miriam's, but Nickel didn't think the man looked like a rodent. In fact, he couldn't put his finger on what kind of animal he was.

The man looked at Nickel's mom, then down at the newspaper in her hand. Then he looked over at Nickel.

"We're looking for an apartment," Nickel said.

The man frowned and began shaking his head. "No," he said. "We're full up."

He started to swing the door shut, but then he hesitated. He cocked an ear as if he'd heard something, then looked back at Nickel. His gaze locked on a spot atop Nickel's head.

"That's Miriam," Nickel said.

Miriam chirped and burrowed deeper into Nickel's hair.

"We're sorry we disturbed you," Nickel's mom said politely to the man. "Let's go," she whispered to Nickel. She tugged at his arm, but he didn't budge.

A tiny smile formed at the corners of the man's lips. "Come in," he said, gesturing for them to enter. "Please. Come right in."

Nickel peeked past the man into the building. The light inside was hazy and blue. He felt himself being drawn in by it, his body being pulled inside, but then suddenly he was stopped short. Something held him back.

"No, thanks," his mom said. It was her arm that was holding him back. She had it stretched across his chest and began backing away from the door, dragging him along with her. "We're sorry we disturbed you."

The man edged forward out of the shadows. He had on a shabby, old, gray robe. The light that had been striking the brass nameplate struck him on the forehead, and he recoiled from it as if it had been a blow to the head. He shaded his eyes and shrunk back into the darkness.

Nickel kept his eyes on the doorway all the way down the alley. Even after his mom had turned him around and was pulling him by the hand behind her, he kept his head twisted around, his chin over his shoulder, looking at the gray door as it swung shut.

And then they were back out on the street.

"Cree-ee-py!" his mom said with a shudder. Her stride was swift as she pulled Nickel along the sidewalk and around a corner.

"There it is!" she said suddenly, pointing up ahead. "There's the café!"

Nickel didn't hear, didn't see. Though his eyes were open, all he could see was what he had seen in the alley: the soft light, the brass nameplate, the gray door, the seashell ear, the man in the robe. The vision persisted, even as his mother dragged him into the café and sat him down on a sequined cushion on the floor by a low table, even as she ordered and as the tea came, steaming and strong-smelling under his nose. He only saw the ear, the light, the man, the name: THE BEASTLY ARMS APARTMENTS. He saw how the man had changed, how his eyes had changed, when he saw —

"Miriam," Nickel murmured, snapping back to the present.

"She's in your pocket," his mom said, lifting her teacup to her lips.

Nickel peered down at Miriam and she rose up and rubbed his nose with hers.

"Keep her out of sight!" Nickel's mom whispered. "People are funny about having R-A-T-S in their restaurants!"

Nickel patted Miriam's head gently, and she settled back down inside his pocket.

The server returned and set a platter on the table between Nickel and his mom. There were pita wedges, black olives, tabouleh salad, hummus, and dolmas on it. "This place has the best food," Nickel's mom said, picking up a dolma with her fingers, "and it's cheap. It's the neighbor-

hood. If this place were uptown, lunch would cost a fortune. But here — I couldn't make this food at home for
what they charge."

"Mom," Nickel asked her. "Why did he ask us in?"

His mom chewed her food, swallowed, then said,
"Who?"

"The man at the Beastly Arms."

"The Beastly Arms?"

"The place at the end of the alley," Nickel said. "That's
what it was called."

"The Beastly Arms," she said to herself, shaking her
head. She picked up a wedge of pita and spooned up some
hummus with it. "I don't know," she said. "He didn't look
very well."

"He said they were full then he looked at Miriam,"
Nickel said. "Then he said, 'Come in.'"

His mom sipped some coffee. She leaned back against
the wall behind her. A circle of light shown on her
through the round café window. The shadow of the
words "Kalamata Café" (which was painted on the window) fell across her chest. She slipped her hand into her

bag and came out with her polaroid. She'd brought it along to shoot any apartments they liked so they could look at them later at home, but had never had to take it out of her purse.

"Be still a minute," she said, bringing it up to her eye, aiming it at Nickel. "You should see your face," she said, and pressed the button. The camera flashed and the motor spat out the undeveloped photograph. "You look like you've seen a ghost."

She slid the photograph across the table to Nickel. It was a smoky, light-blue color. An image was beginning to emerge. Nickel was always amazed by how polaroid film developed in the light. When it was finished, it looked like a picture of a bush baby who'd just seen a ghost.

"Well," his mom said with a deep sigh. "No luck today. I'll check tomorrow's paper. They run new ads on Sundays."

"Do I have to go to dad's tomorrow?" he asked.

His mom nodded. "He's going to pick you up at eleven. He says he has a surprise for you." She rolled her eyes.

Nickel rolled his, too. His dad's surprises often meant a day spent at a mall shopping for clothes, or at a golf tournament, or at the zoo, none of which Nickel looked forward to, especially the zoo. He hated seeing animals in cages.

"But then how will I help you look for an apartment?" he asked.

"Well, I'll look by myself and if I find anything that I think we might like, we'll go back together on Monday, after school."

"Oh!" Nickel said, clamping his hand over his mouth.

"What? What's wrong?"

"I forgot," he said through his fingers. "There's no school on Monday. Remember? It's parent–teacher conference day! You have to go! Remember? I told you!"

"I remember," his mom said, closing her eyes and slightly shaking her head. "I just forgot. I'm meeting your teacher during my lunch hour." She was silent a moment, then she opened her eyes again. "Well, if I find an apartment I like, maybe we can go look at it after the conference. Maybe I can get someone to cover my lab time. If I find something, that is, which I seriously doubt."

The two of them sat quietly, thinking about all of this, when the server returned. "Is everything all right here?" she asked with a smile.

Nickel's mom laughed. "Oh, yes!" she said. "Everything's just perfect!"

6

AFTER lunch, Nickel jumped on the number 46 outbound bus, waved his transit pass at the driver, and took a seat at the back. From there he waved good-bye to his mom, who was standing outside at the corner under the bus stop sign, waving back. She had things to do, she'd said, so she couldn't go with him. The bus pulled away from the curb and Nickel waved until his mom became just another small shape in the geometry of the city.

Inez was sitting on one of the big concrete lions in front of the library when Nickel arrived. She was pretending to ride it like a bucking bronco.

"Howdy, pard!" she called out. Her braids were unbound and danced like octopus tentacles on her head.

"Hi," Nickel said.

They went in through the tall, bronze doors, through the vestibule, and past the circulation desk into the domed central hall. Here, Nickel always stopped and gazed up at the dome high above, watching the dusty light filter in through the doors of the colonnade and fall past him onto the marble floor. Nickel imagined the tiny motes that clung to the dust particles as they floated in the light, so tiny they could not be seen by the naked eye, but alive, just the same, and no doubt enjoying the ride. Without thinking, Nickel's hands went up, cupped, as if checking for rain, and he began to slowly spin in place.

Inez stepped up close behind him and whispered in his ear, "Earth to Nickel. Earth to Nickel. Come in, please." She placed her hands on his arms and pulled them down to his sides. "You can dance with the light later, Space Cadet Dill," she said. "The program's going to start."

She hustled him into the children's books room where Ms. Blackburn gestured for them to hurry along into the auditorium. The white movie screen had been pulled down and metal folding chairs were arranged in curved rows with an aisle down the center. At the back of the hall a film projector was set up. There were two big reels: one empty, one full.

Nickel thought of how he transferred his film from roll to reel in the dark, just as the film in the projector would be transferred — unrolled and rerolled — in the dark. Nickel wandered over to it, hoping he could see the little individual photographs on the film. He turned his head sideways. All he saw was opaque, white plastic leader. He noticed that, like the film in his magazines, but unlike the film on developing reels, the spooled film was allowed to touch itself.

"Will you come on!" Inez yelled across the auditorium. She had found them seats and was waving at him frantically.

Nickel's face turned red, and he hustled down the aisle and took his seat beside her.

"Good afternoon, everyone, and welcome to another of the library's Saturday afternoon film programs," Ms. Blackburn said, standing in front of the screen. The children gradually stopped their chattering and began shushing one another. The noise level remained about the same. Ms. Blackburn folded her hands in front of her and looked reproachfully around the room, her head jerking nervously from side to side. The audience quieted down.

"Today," she went on, "we are going to see some films

made by a French scientist and filmmaker named Jean Painlevé. These films were made in the name of science and were used to look very closely and carefully at various animals, including sea horses, vampire bats, octopi . . ."

"She's an arctic ground squirrel," Nickel whispered to Inez.

"I was wondering," Inez whispered back.

When Ms. Blackburn finished her introduction, she stepped aside and the lights went out. Nickel could see nothing but the stars they had left behind on his retinas. Then the projector came on and the screen lit up. Some words flashed by, then some numbers in circles: a countdown. There was a beep and the screen went dark. Nickel could still see the encircled number one floating in the air before his eyes.

His mom had explained this phenomenon to him once. She said that when the eye sees something and then that something moves or changes or disappears, the eye keeps seeing it as it was for a fraction of a second longer. This is called persistence of vision, she said. Vision persists — it goes on.

Photography, she said, does not see the way the eye does. It doesn't remember. It records. A motion picture camera takes still pictures — dozens per second — and, when projected on a screen, these pictures seem to move. But that is only because the inventors of motion picture photography knew to create a split-second gap — a pause — in between each photograph to allow the human eye to remember. A little black gate closes after each picture, like a camera shutter. When it reopens, the next picture, which advanced while the gate was closed, is projected. The gate closes again, the film advances; the gate opens, the picture is projected; the gate closes, the film advances; gate opens, picture projected; closes, blackness; opens, picture; and on and on and on. The audience sees continuous motion — a movie — but what most people don't know is that the gate is closed for exactly the same length of time that it is open. This means that an audience watching a movie in a theater is actually sitting in the dark half the time, staring at a black screen!

As the first film began — with an enormous black-and-white sea horse bobbing across the screen — Nickel tried to imagine that half of the time, he was not seeing it at all, that the projector was dark, the screen black. But he couldn't. All he could see was the sea horse, bobbing around in its murky underwater world.

When the next film began, color pictures of an octopus spread across the screen, its tentacles groping and curling, and then suddenly, without his summoning it, an image flashed before Nickel's eyes, an image from his mind, from his memory, crowding out the octopi. It was the alley. He saw the gray door, the dusky light, the brass nameplate. The words on the plate ran over and over in his mind: The Beastly Arms, The Beastly Arms. He tried to drive the image from his mind, tried to see the octopus in front of him, but he could only see the gray door opening up, the seashell ears, the big dark eyes looking at Miriam, and it occurred to Nickel that maybe persistence of vision was another way of saying not being able to forget.

Before the program ended, some of the children got restless and started whispering and fidgeting in their seats. A few just couldn't sit any longer and turned around, kneeling on their chairs, reaching up at the tunnel of light and dust overhead. Their fingers cast long, black tentacles on the screen.

When the last film ended, the auditorium lights came back on. The audience, free at last, ran into the aisles, laughing and squealing. Ms. Blackburn stepped in front of the screen and tried to announce the next week's program over the noise, but eventually gave up. She opened the auditorium doors and everyone streamed out into the library.

"Ssssh!" Ms. Blackburn hissed. "Remember where you are!"

Nickel and Inez were the last to leave. They walked solemnly past Ms. Blackburn into the children's book room and then out into the central hall. Nickel was so lost in his thoughts that he didn't even look up at the dome. They went on through the tall, bronze doors and sat down on a marble bench.

"I'm going to be a marine biologist," Inez said suddenly, holding her chin up high.

"I thought you wanted to be a mountain climber," Nickel said.

"I'll be both!" Inez said. She jumped up and turned a quick cartwheel in the small patch of grass behind the bench.

"Do you have to go home now?" Nickel asked.

"What time is it?" Inez asked back, turning another cartwheel back to the bench.

"I don't know," Nickel said. "Three, maybe."

"I have to be home by four-thirty to help Mama make supper. You want to have supper at my house tonight?"

Nickel stood up from the bench. "I want you to see something," he whispered. "A place me and my mom went today."

"Why are you whispering?" Inez said. "What place?"

"It's downtown."

Inez scowled at him. "Will you give me a straight answer! What place?"

"I don't know," Nickel said, squirming a little. "A place. A building. An apartment building."

"An *apartment* building!" Inez said, putting her hands on her hips. "Why would I want to go all the way downtown to see an *apartment* building? I *live* in an apartment building!"

Nickel moved in closer to her. "This one's different," he whispered, then looked around as if someone might be listening. "There's a man there. An old man." He took a deep breath. "I think I might want to interview him."

Inez laughed. "So?" She gave him a shove. "What's the big secret?"

"I don't know," he said, embarrassed. "But there *is* a secret."

Inez gave him a long, hard look. "How do you know?"

Nickel knew why he knew. It was because of Miriam, the way the man had looked at her. It was because of Miriam that the man had invited them in. Maybe he would have told Nickel the secret inside. Maybe he would have shown it to him. In any case, Nickel was positive there was a secret, and he very much wanted to find out what it was.

"I just know," he said to Inez.

"What if it's not a *good* secret?" Inez asked. "What if it's bad?"

"It's not," Nickel said.

"Well, what if it *is*?" Inez asked, pushing her finger into Nickel's chest. "What if his secret is that he eats little boys? Or maybe little rats!" She nudged Miriam in Nickel's pocket with her knuckle.

"Are you coming or not?" Nickel asked.

"Mama would kill me. I'm not supposed to go downtown."

"Okay," Nickel said, "I'll see you later then." He started walking off toward the bus stop. "I don't want you to get in trouble," he said over his shoulder.

"I'm *coming*!" Inez yelled. "She just can't know about it, that's all!"

7

"*YOU* don't know the name of the street?" Inez fumed.

She and Nickel had been circling around downtown for half an hour looking for the Beastly Arms, but Nickel couldn't seem to remember anything: which block, which street, which alley. Nothing looked familiar. The buildings, all old and fallen into disrepair, many with boarded-up windows and doors, were all foreign to him.

"It didn't have a name," Nickel said meekly.

Inez folded her arms and tapped her foot. "So now what do we do?"

"The last apartment we looked at was on 3rd," Nickel said with his eyes closed. He was trying to bring pictures of the morning to his mind's eye, but all he could see was the alley, the gray door. "Mom said she was hungry and that there was a café nearby. We cut down an alley she thought would go through, but it didn't. It was a dead end. At the end of it was the Beastly Arms Apartments." He opened his eyes.

"You're pulling my leg!" Inez said. "*The Beastly Arms?* What is it — an apartment building for monsters!"

"There!" Nickel said suddenly. "There's the Kalamata Café! We're close!"

"So which way do we go?" Inez asked.

Nickel closed his eyes and tried to remember which way he and his mom had walked after they'd left the alley.

"Well, we can't just stand here!" Inez said, giving Nickel a shove. "Open your eyes! You won't find it with your eyes shut!"

She stomped off down the sidewalk. Nickel followed her blindly, his eyes open but not seeing where he was going. He was still looking inward, trying to remember.

They reached the next corner without passing an alley. Inez turned left, pulling Nickel behind her by the hand. They went another block, to the next corner. No alley. They turned left again, walked yet another block without an alley. And again. Inez let go of Nickel's hand.

"Well?" she said, pointing ahead.

Nickel looked up. She was pointing at the Kalamata Café. They were back where they started.

"That's it!" Inez yelled. "I'm history!" She started stomping off again.

"Wait!" Nickel yelled back. "It must be *that* block!" He pointed across the street.

Inez turned around. She set her hands on her hips. "I don't care *what* block it's on! I have to get *home!*"

Nickel rushed up to the round window of the café and pressed his face against it. He cupped his hands around the sides. He remembered there'd been a clock on the wall behind where his mom had sat. Then he turned back to Inez.

"It's only quarter to four!" he called out to her.

Inez snorted and shook her head. "One more block!" she said, holding a forefinger up. *"One!"*

Nickel smiled. "I think it's that one," he said, pointing across the street.

"Better hope you're right," Inez grumbled as she walked toward the corner. Then suddenly she stopped. "Wait!" She backed up a few steps. "What about the map?"

"Map?" Nickel said.

"Yeah," Inez said, starting to grin. "On the bus stop.

On the last corner I saw one of those bus maps. It should have the alley on it!"

She ran off toward the bus stop with Nickel struggling to catch up. The bus stop was an open, clear plastic booth with plastic seats that tilted up vertically when no one was sitting on them. On the inside of one of the walls, encased in plastic, was a map of the city. Someone had spray-painted a thick, black symbol over it, but, luckily, not over the part of town they were in.

"You are here," Inez read, pointing to an arrow on the map.

Nickel studied the little rectangles that stood for city blocks.

"There," Inez said. She pointed at one of the rectangles. It had a thin black line in it that did not go all the way across. "Could that be it?"

Nickel nodded. "Could be."

"Well, let's go look!" Inez said, tugging on his shirt-sleeve.

"You can sure tell who's the boss," said a woman stepping into the booth. She held one of the seats down and sat on it. She was old and gray-haired and wore a flowered scarf tied tightly over her head. Her grin revealed black space in front where teeth used to be. Peeking out of her long, brown raincoat was the scraggly head of a lap dog — a Pekingese. Nickel watched it as Inez dragged him away down the street, not noticing which way they were going, until the dog, and the old woman, disappeared behind the corner of a building. Even still, Nickel kept seeing her toothless grin and the dog's cocked head, its black tongue wagging.

"Is this it?" Inez said, panting.

The image of the dog shattered and Nickel found a different animal before his eyes. It was in the gutter and it didn't move. Its tongue was out and there was dried blood around its mouth. Nickel bent down.

"What is it?" Inez said from behind him.

"A raccoon," Nickel said.

"A *raccoon?*" She knelt down beside him. "What's it doing *here?*"

"Raccoons live in cities sometimes," Nickel said. "They only come out late at night, so people don't see them very much." He reached down and touched the animal's bristly gray fur.

"Don't *touch* it!" Inez said.

Nickel didn't listen. He ran his hand down the animal's side to its black-and-white striped tail.

"Would you leave it alone?" Inez said. "It probably has diseases!"

"I wish I could have seen it when it was still alive," Nickel said under his breath. He looked up and saw cars streaming by in both directions. "It didn't stand a chance around here."

"Will you just forget about that," Inez said, pulling on his shirtsleeve. "Look! I think I found it! The alley!"

Nickel stood up slowly, his eyes still on the raccoon. Inez grasped his shoulders firmly and whirled him around.

"Well?" she said. "Is that it or not?"

They were standing at the entrance to the alley. Though it was hours later, the light had the same quality:

soft, like twilight. The gray door still stood far at the end, its brass nameplate glowing.

"That's it," Nickel said.

"Well, knock," Inez said when they had reached the door.

Nickel just stood there, lost in thought.

"Oh, for crying out loud!" Inez said, and rapped hard on the door.

"There's a doorbell," Nickel whispered, pointing to it.

Inez groaned and pressed it. "What's the matter with you?" she hissed.

Nickel didn't hear her. He was facing the door, but not seeing it. He was seeing the man's face: his large black eyes, his wrinkles, his pale skin, the seashells. The door was still closed, but Nickel saw him.

Inez rang the bell again. "What am I doing?" she muttered to herself. "Mama's going to kill me." She pounded on the door with her fist. "Hello?" she yelled. "Anybody home?"

Miriam rose up on her hind legs in Nickel's pocket,

peeking her nose out over the edge. She sniffed at the air, then began to chatter.

"She probably smells rats," Inez said with disgust. "I bet they're all over the place around here."

"Who is it?" a voice said from behind the door.

Miriam stopped chattering. So did Inez.

"It's N-Nicholas Dill, s-sir," Nickel stammered. "I w-was here b-b-before!"

A few seconds passed. There was no sound. Even the noise from the street behind them seemed to lull. Then the doorknob turned, and the gray door began to open. The man did not hide this time. He stepped into the opening, still in his robe.

"Well, hello again, young man," he said. "And who have you brought with you this time?" He looked over at Inez.

"This is my friend, Inez," Nickel said.

The man extended his hand to her. Inez took it firmly and shook it. "Charmed," she said. "And who might you be?"

The man smiled. "I might be Julius Beastly," he said.

"Oh, I get it," Inez said. "You own the place."

Mr. Beastly smiled again, then looked back at Nickel. "Are you still apartment-hunting?" he asked.

Nickel nodded.

"Well, then, come in," Mr. Beastly said, opening the door wide.

Nickel stepped by him into the building. Inez remained where she was.

"Where you going, Mr. Dill?" she asked sharply.

Nickel stopped and looked back at her. She was scowling at him.

"What?" he whispered.

Inez blinked as if she couldn't believe him. "I sincerely doubt your mama tells you it's okay to go ahead into strangers' houses!" She set her hands on her hips.

In truth, Nickel's mom had told him never to go *anywhere* with strangers, but for some reason, the thought hadn't come to his mind.

"I assure you, Inez," Mr. Beastly said, "no harm will come to you here."

"That's what they all say!" Inez said, crossing her arms.

"Nickel can go in if he wants to. He can make up his own mind — if he has one." She glowered at him. "But I'm staying right here!"

Nickel didn't like to hear her say that. Inez always made such good decisions. He always made bad ones. It made him think that maybe he shouldn't go in. But he had to. Something was pulling him in.

Maybe, he thought, *it's a bad thing that's pulling me in.* He wouldn't let himself believe it.

"That's fine," Mr. Beastly said to Inez, with a smile. "We'll be right back." He started to close the door.

"Leave it open!" Inez said. "I want to see! I can yell real loud, you know!"

"I bet you can," Mr. Beastly said. "We'll just be in there — in the lobby." He pointed inside.

Inez leaned her head cautiously into the doorway. The light inside looked dim and hazy. "Looks spooky to me," she said. She looked up at Mr. Beastly. He was still smiling at her. "Mama says most bad people grin a lot," she said.

"Sorry," Mr. Beastly said, covering his mouth with his hand.

"I guess I better go in," Inez said sternly. "I have to look out for Nickel. Most times he doesn't know *where* he's going!"

Nickel was glad she was coming, but didn't like to think that he needed looking out for — not, at least, by someone his own age. Still, it made him feel good knowing Inez was worried about him. He just hoped nothing bad happened. It would be all his fault.

"Fine," Mr. Beastly said. "I'm proud to have such a wise and conscientious visitor."

"Leave that door open!" Inez said as she started to step inside. "That way his mom won't have to knock. She'll be by any minute, you know."

Nickel understood why Inez was lying. His mom wasn't coming. Inez just wanted Mr. Beastly to think she was.

"And remember," Inez said, "I can scream like a banshee!"

"I'll remember," Mr. Beastly said. "Like a banshee."

"You go first," Inez said.

"Of course. This way."

Nickel followed first, then Inez stepped in slowly, keeping her eye on the door, and scanning the area for dangers.

The lobby was small and square with a very high ceiling, as high as the one in the library vestibule, though not as high as the domed hall. There were no windows whatsoever, only a small skylight high above — it must have been at least thirty feet overhead. Nickel watched dust particles dancing in its beam. The walls of the room were bare. The graying white paint was cracked and peeling. The floor was wooden and dusty. In the center of the room sat a wooden table with four wooden chairs, all covered in cobwebs and a layer of dust. In the corner there was a staircase leading up to who knew where. It vanished into darkness.

Nickel was so lost in looking that he hadn't noticed that Mr. Beastly had approached him. He leaned forward and scratched Miriam on the head.

"I see you brought your little friend with you," Mr. Beastly said.

Nickel jumped. "Her name is M-Miriam," he said.

The man laughed. "So you said before. That's a very good name for a Merriam's kangaroo rat."

Nickel gaped up at him. No one had ever known where he'd gotten Miriam's name from before.

"It smells like Miriam's box in here!" Inez said with disgust. She was standing tentatively in the lobby's doorway, as if she was ready to bolt at any second.

"Please sit," Mr. Beastly said, gesturing for Nickel to take a seat.

Nickel pulled out a chair, wincing at the sound it made as it scraped against the floor. Mr. Beastly sat opposite him.

"So where did you get your little friend?" he asked.

"Inez?" Nickel asked, looking at her across the room. She was edging slowly toward them. "At school, I guess."

Mr. Beastly grinned. "No, I meant Miriam."

"Oh," Nickel said. He raised his hand up to her and she scrambled out of his pocket, down his arm onto the table, and then skittishly across the tabletop to Mr. Beastly. Mr. Beastly eased his hand closer, and she gave it a good sniffing.

"I found her in the park," Nickel said. "Her leg was

hurt. There were a lot of dogs around, so I took her home."

"What did your mother say about that?" Mr. Beastly said, playing with Miriam with his finger.

Nickel shrugged. "She didn't mind. She said not to let Mr. Youdle find out."

"Mr. Youdle?"

"He's our landlord," Nickel said. "He doesn't allow animals in the building."

"What your Mr. Youdle doesn't understand," Mr. Beastly said, "is that — whether he's aware of it or not — all of his tenants are animals! Even your Mr. Youdle himself!"

Nickel smiled. He was surprised he'd never thought of that before.

"I bet she's easy to keep," Mr. Beastly said, smiling down at Miriam. "Some seeds. A few nuts. She doesn't need water. She doesn't urinate."

Nickel was impressed that he knew so much about kangaroo rats. No one, not even his mom, had ever known that they get all the moisture they need from their food and that they rarely, if ever, have to pee. Most people were afraid to hold Miriam for fear she'd piddle on them — like she was a tortoise or something.

"Do you keep her in a cage?" Mr. Beastly asked.

Nickel shook his head. "I made her a nest out of a box. She can get out if she wants. She sleeps in my pocket a lot. At night, she runs around in my room. I think she gets lonely."

Mr. Beastly nodded. He looked down at Miriam, who was tickling his finger with her paws. He turned his hand over and opened it. In his palm was a pumpkin seed. Nickel gasped. Miriam leaped at the seed and tucked it into her cheek. Then she darted back across the table, hopped up Nickel's shirtfront, and settled back into his pocket to work on the seed.

"What was it?" Inez asked, inching closer.

"A treat," Mr. Beastly said to her. He turned back to Nickel. "So you and your mother are looking for an apartment?"

Nickel nodded vacantly.

Mr. Beastly ran his hand over the wispy hair on his

head, then rose slowly from his chair. He paced back and forth across the room a few times, rubbing his beard. He wasn't wearing shoes. He was barefoot. And bare-legged. His feet were filthy.

"I do have an apartment," Mr. Beastly said as if to himself. "It needs paint."

Nickel looked at Inez. He didn't know what to ask.

"How many bedrooms?" Inez asked.

Mr. Beastly looked over at her. "Two," he said. "Plus a kitchen, of course, and a dining room, a bath, and a sitting room."

"How much?" Inez asked, her hands on her hips.

"Much?" Mr. Beastly asked.

"Yes, how much? You know — rent?"

"Oh," Mr. Beastly said with a worried expression, "I hadn't thought of that."

"You hadn't thought of that?" Inez said. She gave Nickel a sideways glance.

"How does two hundred sound?" Mr. Beastly said.

"A week?" Inez asked.

"A month."

"A month!" Inez yelped.

"Too much?"

"Can we see it?" Nickel asked.

"I'm not going anywhere with this guy!" Inez said.

"It's a real mess," Mr. Beastly said to Nickel. "I could probably show it to you in, say, a few days."

"Can I bring my mom to see it on Monday? We don't have school on Monday."

"Monday," the man said to himself. He rubbed his beard again. "What's today?" he asked in a very quiet voice, then glanced over at Inez. Her mouth had fallen open.

"It's Saturday," Nickel said politely.

"Oh, that's soon," Mr. Beastly said, pacing again. "Monday." He shook his head. "That's very soon."

"What if we call on Monday and, if it's ready, we come and see it?" Nickel asked.

Mr. Beastly looked over at Inez again.

"Get out!" she said. "You don't have a *phone!*"

He grinned sheepishly and shook his head.

Inez stomped across the room to Nickel. She leaned

over and hissed in his ear, "Let's get out of here! Right now! This guy's nuts!"

"Come by on Monday," Mr. Beastly said in a voice much deeper and stronger than he'd been using. He sounded more sure of himself. "I'll have it ready," he said, and gave a firm nod of his head.

Nickel stood up. "Okay," he said. "I'll bring my mom."

"Fine," the man said, his voice a little less confident. He tightened his robe around himself.

"Let's go!" Inez said to Nickel. She began tugging him toward the door by his shirtsleeve.

"See you Monday!" Nickel called out as he was dragged away.

Mr. Beastly waved at them. "Monday," he said to himself.

8

"*I* am *dead!*" Inez said as they reached the street. "What time is it?"

Nickel noticed that the light was soft and orange. It was the golden hour. "I don't know. After five," he said.

"After five!" Inez shrieked. "I am *double* dead!"

A bus went past then and, suddenly, she sprinted ahead, waving frantically and yelling, "The bus! The bus!" It stopped at the corner, made a PSSSsssssh sound, and its double doors opened. When Inez caught up to it, she boarded then began gesturing madly at the driver and pointing down the sidewalk in Nickel's direction. When he reached the door, huffing and puffing, the driver glowered at him. It took Nickel a minute before he was able to dig out his pass. He didn't have enough breath left to thank the driver for waiting. The bus lurched forward and Nickel tumbled down the aisle. Inez caught him and dragged him into the seat next to her. The two of them leaned back against their seats, panting and staring up at the ceiling. The lights were on.

"You're coming with," Inez said when she'd finally caught her breath. "I'm not going in alone. This is *your* fault!"

"Okay, okay," Nickel said, nodding.

"Mama won't kill me in front of you," Inez said. "Just tell her we stayed late at the library. Don't tell her we went downtown, whatever you do! She'll ground me to my room forever!"

"I won't," Nickel said.

They both took a deep breath and let it out. Nickel watched the city lights flickering past the large, rectangular windows of the bus. It reminded him of a strip of film.

"I had to tell the man what *day* it is!" Inez said.

"No you didn't," Nickel said, still looking out the windows. "I did."

"You're not really going back there, are you?"

Nickel glanced over at her. He always trusted her. She always made the right decisions. But he had to go back. Something in his stomach told him to.

"Uh-huh," he said.

        ❦   ❦   ❦

Inez unlocked the front door of her building and pushed it open. She and Nickel were halfway up the first flight of stairs before it had clicked shut behind them. By the fourth floor, they were wheezing and holding their sides. By the sixth, their legs were wobbly. When they finally reached Inez's door — on the eighth — they took a moment to catch their breath and compose themselves for what lay ahead.

"Remember," Inez whispered. "No downtown."

Nickel nodded.

Inez took one last deep breath, then opened the door.

"Inez?" a voice called out.

Inez stood still a moment, trying to detect her mother's mood from the grain of her voice. Then she called back, "Yes, Mama! It's me! Me and Nickel!"

Her mother appeared at the end of the hall. She was rubbing her hands with a dish towel. Her sleeves were rolled up. Her apron was dusted with flour. Her expression was cross.

"At this hour, I figured you for your papa!" she said.

She was wearing blue jeans and a yellow button-down

shirt under her checked apron. Her skin was brown like Inez's, though lighter, her hair as black and curly. Instead of wearing it in braids, though, she wore it cut close to her scalp. Her ears were small and round, her eyes large and dark, her face slender and triangular. Ms. Willamina was a wallaby.

"I'm sorry I'm late, Mama," Inez said. She waited for her mother to press for an explanation before volunteering a fib.

"Well, supper's about on the table," Ms. Willamina said. "Do me a favor and get Cecil cleaned up, will you?" She turned and walked back toward the kitchen.

"Yes, Mama!" Inez called after her. "Right away!" She winked at Nickel.

"You're welcome to stay and eat with us if you like, Nickel," Ms. Willamina called from the kitchen.

"Thank you!" Nickel called back, then he whispered to Inez, "I better go."

"Oh, no!" Inez hissed at him. "Stay until Papa gets home!"

It was dark out when they'd entered the building.

Nickel figured it must be near six o'clock, and by the time he ran home . . .

"Come on!" Inez whispered. "You *owe* me!"

"Inez!" Ms. Willamina called from the kitchen. "Stop your dawdling and help me with your brother!"

"Yes, Mama!" Inez yelled. She looked at Nickel with big, pleading eyes.

"Okay," Nickel said, wishing he were brave enough to say otherwise.

Inez grabbed his hand and dragged him down the hall.

Cecil was in his high chair, his face, hair, and ears covered with orange goop. He had a face like his father's — like a mink's — only with beadier eyes and a pointier nose and a much more mischievous look. Cecil was a coatimundi. He banged one chubby fist down onto his plastic plate and the other on the side of his own head. He was coordinated that way.

"Oh, Cecil!" Inez said, rushing to him. She took the plate away and began wiping his face with a terry cloth mitt that had been left on the table for just that purpose. Cecil laughed and beat on his chrome tray with both fists.

"Cecil!" Inez snapped. "I am trying to wipe your face!"

"How's your mama?" Ms. Willamina asked Nickel. She was standing at the stove stirring chopped onions and garlic in a pan.

"Fine," Nickel said, which is what he always said if someone asked him that.

"That's good," Ms. Willamina said quietly. "I sure like Maud. She's a fine person. You're lucky to have her."

"Their landlord raised their rent again, Mama," Inez said, holding Cecil's clenched fists in her hands. "They're looking around for a new place."

"Well, that's a shame!" Ms. Willamina said. She stopped stirring and pointed her wooden spoon at Nickel. "What about that father of yours? Why doesn't he help out?"

Nickel shrugged. He didn't know. He didn't understand about money and child support and making ends meet and all the other things his mom and dad argued about. He saw his dad one Sunday a month and three weeks in August and his mom all the rest of the time. He couldn't see how money figured into it. If anything, it seemed that his dad gave his mom money to keep him so that he didn't have to.

"There's your papa," Ms. Willamina said to Inez, though Nickel hadn't heard anything. "That you, Robert?" she called out.

"It's either me or someone just as handsome," Mr. Willamina's voice answered.

Nickel heard the front door close. He caught Inez's eye. "Well?" he whispered. Inez nodded.

"I better get going now," Nickel said to Ms. Willamina. "I don't want to be late."

Ms. Willamina shot Inez a glare. "No," she said meaningfully. "You don't want your mama to worry."

"Well, look at this!" Mr. Willamina said as he appeared in the doorway. "A hero's welcome! And all for little old me?" He pretended to be embarrassed. "I suppose there are some very expensive welcome home gifts around here somewhere." He opened the lid of the flour canister on the counter and peeked inside. Inez giggled; then Cecil did.

Mr. Willamina was wearing jeans, sneakers, and a blue smock. Inez's parents were both nurses and worked at the same clinic downtown. That was where they'd met. They worked different shifts now so one of them could always be home with Cecil.

"And how are my beautiful children this evening?" Mr. Willamina said, kissing Inez's braids. He lifted the freshly wiped Cecil from his chair. "Happy and attending to your mama's every need?"

Ms. Willamina snorted.

Mr. Willamina went over and kissed his wife on the ear. He seemed much taller than her, but they were actually about the same height. He only appeared taller because of his long neck and torso — because he was a mink and she, a wallaby. Nickel had never known anyone who smiled as much as Inez's dad.

"And how are you, Nickel?" Mr. Willamina asked.

"Hi, Mr. Willamina," Nickel said.

"What's that sleeping in your pocket?" Mr. Willamina asked.

Nickel smiled. He knew Mr. Willamina knew.

"Nickel was just saying he has to go," Ms. Willamina said. "He doesn't want to worry his mama, not like some little girls I know." She gave her husband a sidelong look.

"Oh!" Mr. Willamina said, pretending to be shocked. He looked down at Inez and pretended to be cross. "Did you worry your sweet mama?" he asked, waving his finger at her.

Inez laughed.

"Didn't I tell you *never* to worry your sweet mama?" he went on, hiding a smile. "Didn't I tell you that only I, and I alone, get to worry your sweet mama?"

"Oh, thank you," Ms. Willamina said. "Thank you so much. Now, would you kindly collect your children and wash them up for supper?"

"Come, children," Mr. Willamina said. "Come on now with your papa. It is your sweet mama's wish that we —"

"Oh, get out of here!" Ms. Willamina said, waving her spoon over her head.

"Uh-oh! She's snapping! She's snapping!" Mr. Willamina said, acting panicked. "Get out of the kitchen, children! Get out of this kitchen! Your mama's snapping! She's snapping!"

He hustled Inez and Cecil out, and Nickel could hear them clomping down the hall to the bathroom.

"Good-bye, Ms. Willamina," Nickel said.

"Good-bye, Nickel." She looked down at him. "You tell your father to do the right thing. Okay?"

"Okay," Nickel said.

9

AS Nickel neared the door to his apartment, he heard cabinets doors inside being slammed. He wished he had Inez with him.

"There you are!" his mom said as he opened the door. She looked more scared than angry, though sometimes that was worse. "Do you know what time it is?"

Nickel looked at the clock over the fridge. It was a quarter to seven.

"Where have you been?" his mom asked.

"At Inez's," Nickel said. It wasn't everywhere he'd been, but he would save the rest for later — when she'd calmed down.

"You could've called!" his mom said, placing her palm against her forehead. She closed her eyes and took a deep breath. "Call next time, please."

"Okay," Nickel said. "I'm sorry."

"Your dinner's on the table."

Nickel nodded and ducked past her into the kitchen. He gave his hands a quick rinse in the sink and sat down.

He was starving. On the table there was a plate of ravioli, a small dish with a green salad, and a glass of water. Across the table was another plate, the ravioli on it nibbled at, and an emptied glass of wine. The bottle was in the center of the table. Nickel dove into his ravioli. They were stuffed with ricotta cheese.

His mom sat down across from him and refilled her glass halfway.

"Chin-chin," she said, raising it up.

Nickel set his fork down and raised his water glass. "Chin-chin," he said, and clinked her glass. They each sipped, then Nickel went back to his meal.

His mom set her elbow on the table and rested her chin on her palm. "How was the program?" she asked.

"Good," Nickel said between bites.

"Did you know the filmmaker?"

Nickel shook his head. "His name was Jean Painlevé." He said it the way Ms. Blackburn had: Zhon Pon-le-VAY. He always paid special attention to directors because he knew his mom would want to know.

His mom smiled. "Sea horses?" she asked.

"And octopi," Nickel mumbled with his mouth full.

"I've seen them," his mom said dreamily. "I can close my eyes and still see them." She closed her eyes.

"A sea horse is actually a fish," Nickel said. "It's related to the perch. The weird thing about sea horses is the males hatch the eggs. They have pouches, like kangaroos and opossums."

"I wonder if the males share the *rearing* of the sea foals," his mom said with a smirk.

Nickel knew she was talking about his dad.

"Would you like to look at photographs tonight?" his mom asked, taking a bite of salad. "I did some printing this afternoon."

Nickel nodded, then, suddenly remembering what he had done that afternoon, stared up at her.

"What?" she asked. "What's wrong?"

Nickel swallowed the ravioli in his mouth. He hadn't really chewed it. He took a sip of water. Then he said, "I went back to the Beastly Arms." Right after the words left his mouth he wished he could have them back. He was positive his mother would be furious and forbid him from ever going there again. She certainly would never agree to go and look at the apartment.

"When?" his mom asked. She didn't seem angry yet. Just confused.

"After the program," Nickel said.

"Is that why you were so late?"

"N-No," Nickel stammered. He didn't want to contradict what he'd said earlier.

"Were you at Inez's or not?" Now she was getting angry.

"Yes," Nickel said, whining a little. "She wanted me to go in with her. She was supposed to be home at four-thirty. We got lost downtown and so she was late."

His mom leaned forward across the table. "*Inez* went with you?"

Nickel shrunk in his chair. This wasn't going well at all.

"Did her mom know?"

Nickel shook his head so slightly his mom almost didn't see it.

"Oh, Nickel," she sighed, leaning back in her chair.

"I'll have to tell her. You do know that downtown is off limits, don't you? You and Inez aren't allowed down there without permission, without supervision."

Nickel hung his head. "I know."

Neither of them spoke for a while. Nickel didn't eat. He stared out the window. Mr. Ojeda was washing dishes.

"Look," his mom said finally, "I won't talk to the Willaminas about it. I'm just glad you're both home safe and sound. But you are not to go down there again. And you are to respect the Willaminas' wishes. Understand?" She pointed her finger at him.

He nodded.

"And stay away from that place — that man," she said with a shudder. "He gives me the creeps."

"He has an apartment for rent," Nickel blurted out. "I said you'd come and see it." He winced.

"Well, I'm not going to!" his mom said. She wasn't angry. She was just putting her foot down. "Maybe you should check with me before you tell someone what I'll do!" She started to stand up.

"The rent's two hundred dollars a month," Nickel said.

She sat back down.

"Two hundred?" she said. "It must be a rattrap!"

"It has two bedrooms and a sitting room and a dining room," Nickel said.

"A sitting room?" his mom said. "No apartments have sitting rooms! No apartments we can afford, anyway."

Nickel shrugged.

"Two hundred!" his mom said to herself. "He must be insane!"

"He's nice," Nickel said.

"Two bedrooms, you said?"

"Uh-huh," Nickel said. He could see she was weakening.

"Two hundred dollars? You're sure he said hundred? Not thousand?"

Nickel nodded.

His mom looked away. She shook her head, mumbled to herself, then she looked back at Nickel. "When did you say we'd come?"

"Monday afternoon."

"Nickel!" his mom said, rolling her eyes. "I have a conference with your teacher then!"

Nickel covered his mouth with his hand. He hadn't thought of that! Why was he always forgetting things!

"What time did you tell him?" his mom asked.

"I didn't," Nickel said, lowering his hand. "He just said afternoon."

His mom thought for a second. "Well," she said, "Maybe we could squeeze it in after the conference. It'd be a tight squeeze, though. I might get someone to cover my lab."

"We could do it!" Nickel said.

His mom nodded. "All right," she said. "I'm just desperate enough."

Nickel smiled.

"I'm glad that pleases you," she said, scowling a little. "Don't get your hopes up. I'm not saying he's not crazy, or that the apartment isn't a dive. I'm just saying we'll see. We'll go and look."

Nickel nodded. Then, his appetite returned, he speared two ravioli and stuffed them into his mouth.

ⓢ　　ⓢ　　ⓢ

After the dishes, Nickel and his mom settled down on the couch with a big, flat box of photographs. Miriam sat on the armrest by Nickel, gnawing on some sunflower seeds he'd given her.

The photographs were eleven-by-seventeen-inch black-and-white prints. They still smelled of the darkroom. The top one in the box was of a man coming out of a pizzeria. He wore a sea captain's hat and a white raincoat and was hunched over, biting into a slice of pizza, trying not to let it spill down his front. Standing to his right, and probably unseen by him, were two girls about Nickel's age, leaning against the building. They were laughing very hard. Nickel decided that they weren't laughing at the man because they wouldn't have had enough time to react to him. He had only just stepped outside.

"I was focusing on the girls," Nickel's mom said. "The man walked out just as I hit the shutter. I didn't plan it."

"You must have been standing in the street," Nickel said.

"Why?"

"That's Angelo's," Nickel said, pointing at the pizzeria. "You couldn't have gotten all of this in unless you were in the street."

His mom smiled. "Maybe I used a wide-angle."

"You didn't. If you were that close and used a wide-angle, things would look distorted. The sidewalk would curve."

"Good work, Sherlock," his mom said.

"You shouldn't stand in the street and take pictures," Nickel said. "It's dangerous."

"You shouldn't walk down the street with your head in the clouds," his mom said.

She lifted the photograph out of the box and set it face down into the lid. The next picture was of a woman sitting on a dirty blanket on the sidewalk, her back against a building, a plastic basket in her lap. There were some coins in the basket. Beside the woman stood a little girl, her arms upstretched, her palms up. She was straining so hard upward that her arms pressed her cheeks together, causing her lips to pucker.

"She's a swordfish," Nickel said, "jumping out of the ocean."

The last one was of a woman sitting alone at a bus stop. She was old and gray-haired and wore a flowered scarf on her head. It was the woman Nickel had seen downtown, the one with the Pekingese poking out of her raincoat. Nickel looked more closely and saw just the tip of the dog's black nose and the tip of its black tongue peeking out between the raincoat's buttons.

"That's a Pekingese," he said.

"You think so?" his mom said, looking closer.

"Not the woman." He pointed to the nose and tongue. "I've seen her before. She keeps her dog in her coat."

"I see her all the time," his mom said. "I don't think she has a home."

"She's a tortoise," Nickel said.

"But a tortoise has a home. It has its shell."

"That's not its home. Everyone has a shell. A tortoise's is just harder."

His mom set the photograph into the lid, then set the

bottom of the box into the top and flipped the box back over.

"I'm going to go to bed and read," she said, wrapping her arm around Nickel. "What are you going to do?"

"I think I'll do my homework."

"What's the assignment?"

"To think."

"Oh," his mom said. "Well, good luck." She kissed his head. "See you in the morning." And she went off to her room.

Nickel stretched out on the couch. The spot where his mom had been was warm against the back of his legs. Miriam scampered off the armrest, down over Nickel's shoulders, and settled down on his chest. She spit a seed out of her mouth into her paws and gnawed it.

Nickel's eyes fell on the framed photograph on the wall facing him. It was a picture he knew by heart. It had hung there for longer than they had lived at the Gardenview Apartments. It had hung in every living room in every house he and his mom had ever lived in, even when they lived with his dad. He could conjure it up in his mind's eye no matter where he was or what he was doing. All he had to do was close his eyes and think of it. He could even see a ghost image of it with his eyes open if he chose to.

The photograph was taken by Henri Cartier-Bresson, one of Nickel's mom's favorite photographers. The picture was of a group of children, all boys, playing together in a narrow street. It had been taken through a large, cloud-shaped hole in a cracked, crumbling wall. The street was covered with rubble. One of the boys stood at the right of the picture near a wall that looked as if a great beast had taken several bites out of it. The sockets of this boy's eyes were very dark, almost black, but even so it was plain that, when the picture was taken, he had been looking through the big hole at the photographer, who was on the other side of the wall with his camera. This boy, the only one who seemed aware a photograph was being taken, was Nickel's favorite.

Nickel shut his eyes. He could see the boys in the street

on the inside of his eyelids. He looked at each one in turn — the one with the hoop, the one with the crutches, the one with the black arm band, his favorite one — wondering about each one's life, each one's mom, each one's dad. He fell asleep wondering about them.

10

NICKEL'S dad called the next morning to tell him to be ready and on the curb at ten o'clock. He was to wear clean clothes and to leave Miriam behind. The restaurant where they would be having brunch didn't allow rodents.

When the car came by, Nickel climbed into the back.

"You look nice," Julie said, twisting around in her seat.

"Thanks," Nickel said.

"No rat, right?" his dad asked.

"Right."

"Good man."

They had breakfast uptown. The waiters wore white shirts and black ties. Nickel ate two Belgian waffles with berries and whipped cream that cost as much as five hundred feet of black-and-white film.

Then came the surprise: They were taking him antiquing. Nickel didn't know what that was, but he learned soon enough that it was just another form of shopping. The three of them browsed through the Rusty Kettle, then through Curiouser & Curiouser Collectibles, then through Mabel's Attic. They went through a dozen stores in all. When they'd finished, Nickel's dad packed his and Julie's purchases (an old stove-top toaster, an old embroidered ottoman, and an old candy dish in the shape of a whale) into the trunk, and they headed back to the Gardenview.

"Been working on your mom?" his dad asked when they got there.

Nickel shrugged in the backseat.

"Well, keep at her. I need your help, son."

Nickel looked down at the floor mat. "Okay," he said.

"Oh, I almost forgot," his dad said, and handed Nickel a small paper sack with the words THE RUSTY KETTLE on it.

Nickel opened it and found an antique light meter inside. It was made of black metal with a frosted glass bulb.

"Thanks!" Nickel said, surprised.

He held it up to the window and watched the needle dance back and forth. Though he never used a light meter, he knew how one worked. In a second or two the needle settled on a recommended exposure setting.

"The guy said it still works perfectly," Nickel's dad said. "Now maybe you can take pictures of something other than clouds."

Nickel nodded. "Maybe."

His mom had spent the day apartment-hunting, without success.

"We may be staying here and paying Mr. Youdle's price after all," she said over dinner.

"There's still the Beastly Arms," Nickel reminded her.

"Yeah," his mom said, rolling her eyes. "The Beastly Arms."

The next morning was another of those mornings when Nickel and his mom just couldn't seem to get out the door. When they finally did, they rushed through the gray drizzle to Kleindienst's Bakery, picked up muffins and coffee and hot cocoa to go, then dashed toward the subway, eating and sipping at red lights. The wind in the tunnel shot straight through Miriam's bones. She shivered in Nickel's pocket. Nickel gulped down the rest of his cocoa on the train. It had gone cold.

The plan was for Nickel to go to the college with his mom. While she taught, he would work in the darkroom, printing the negatives he had developed on Friday. Then, during her lunch hour, they'd go to his school for her conference with Mr. Kirkaby. His mom wasn't sure yet if there would be time to go to the Beastly Arms. She'd have to find someone to cover her afternoon lab.

Once in Room C, Nickel found that his negatives had been taken out of the drying cabinet and cut and put into plastic sleeves. His mom must have done it for him the day before while she was there printing.

Nickel mixed up his chemicals — the soup, the stop bath, the fix — and poured them into printing trays. Then he slipped the sleeve of negatives into a printing frame, glossy side up, and set the frame on the enlarger's baseboard. He unlocked his mom's private drawer (he had a copy of her key on his key ring), and removed a box of photo paper. After checking the enlarger's settings, he flicked off the overhead light. The safety light came on. The room glowed red.

Nickel removed a sheet of photo paper from the box

and slipped it into the printing frame, glossy side up, under the negatives. He closed the glass cover, sandwiching the negatives and the paper together, then switched on the enlarger. A circle of light shone down on the baseboard, completely illuminating the printing frame. The light began in the enlarger's lamp, passed through its lens, through the air, through the frame's glass cover, through the plastic sleeve, through the negatives (strongly where the negative was light, weakly where it was dark) to the photo paper, where it was altering the silver halide crystals in the paper, "telling" the paper what the clouds had looked like, though the paper didn't appear changed.

"The pictures are in the paper," his mom explained once, "The same way a plant is inside a seed. Add water and nutrients and sunshine and — voilà! — it appears." (To photo paper, though, you add developer, stop bath, and fix.)

After five seconds, the enlarger lamp clicked off. Nickel opened the printing frame, slipped the paper out and slid it into the soup, tamping it down with rubber-tipped tongs. Within a few seconds, the image began to emerge, ghostlike at first, then gradually more and more defined. The seed had sprouted. When the print was fully developed, Nickel lifted it out with the tongs and transferred it to the stop bath. He counted for twenty seconds then moved it to the fix. A few minutes later, he switched the overhead light back on. There were the musk ox, the mud puppy catching a ball, the shrew that threw it, the swooping barn owl, each of them only thirty-five millimeters wide, all of them together on one sheet of paper — a contact sheet.

Normally at this point, Nickel would decide which of the pictures he liked well enough to enlarge to eight-and-a-half-by-eleven-inch photographs. He usually skipped repetitions. He had lots of sheep, for example. Sometimes, pictures were hard to make out. What looked like a cicada munching a leaf at Flood Hill Park didn't always look like one on a contact sheet. And then sometimes he didn't make enlargements simply because he wasn't particularly fond of the image. He couldn't always say why.

This day he didn't make any enlargements. He just didn't feel like it. He hung the contact sheet on the line to dry, dumped his chemicals into the sink, gathered his things together, and locked up. On the notepad on the darkroom door, he wrote:

M.—

Went to the Library to do homework.

—N..

He ran a finger along the spines of the books in the 590s: beetles, butterflies, fish, snakes, birds, frogs, turtles, bats, whales, elephants, bears, apes. He pulled down a big book called *The Primates* and carried it to a soft chair by the window. He let the book fall open in his lap, and it happened to open on a photograph of a man. He was standing up straight, his arms hanging down at his sides, his gaze straight ahead into the camera. He was neither smiling nor frowning, and he had no clothes on. It seemed strange to see a man like that. Nickel never saw men like that in the real world. He'd never even seen his dad that way. He'd seen himself, of course, in the bathroom mirror at home, but he wasn't a man. Not yet.

On the facing page was a photograph of a naked woman. The man and the woman had the same skin color (a light, pinkish tan) and about the same shape. They were slim and tall and about the same age — younger than his mom and dad, closer to Julie's age, Nickel decided. In his mind's eye, he replaced the man with Mr. Youdle, the woman with Inez's mom, then giggled at the sight of it. Then he imagined Sixto and Agatha the pie lady. He giggled harder. Then he imagined Gwendolyn and Mr. Beastly. He didn't giggle. He closed the book and turned to the window.

He didn't see the gray drizzle, the courtyard with the fountain in the center. He saw Mr. Beastly, without his robe. It didn't seem silly. What was wrong with not wearing clothes anyway? No other animal wore clothes. No other animal made clothes. No other animal needed clothes. Nickel never thought it was strange to see himself naked. Sometimes it seemed strange to see himself clothed — in school pictures, for example, or reflected in shop windows. It seemed to Nickel that people were ashamed of being animals and he couldn't understand why.

"What's wrong with being an animal?" he muttered to himself.

He was sleeping in the chair by the window, the book still open in his lap to the same page, when his mom came for him. She didn't give the pictures a second thought; she knew her son. She shook him gently, helped him to his feet, then led him, still half asleep, toward the exit.

Nickel didn't awaken fully until the subway train screeched up to the platform.

"Lynn's going to cover me," his mom told him once they were aboard. "But I have to be back for my two-forty."

Nickel watched the blackness flickering past as the train surged through the tunnel. He set his hand over Miriam in his pocket. Her heart was beating a mile a minute.

They arrived at school just in time. Nickel's mom left him in a chair in the hall outside his classroom, saying, "This won't take long."

Nickel wasn't particularly glad to be sitting there with nothing to do while his mom and his teacher were inside discussing him. He peeked in his pocket at Miriam. She was sound asleep. The train ride had worn her out. It would be wrong to wake her just because he felt lonely and restless. He wished Inez were there. With Inez, the time would fly by and Nickel wouldn't even care what Mr. Kirkaby was saying about him.

Nickel began to notice that the voices coming from his classroom were getting louder. It almost sounded as if his mom and Mr. Kirkaby were arguing. But then the voices grew very loud, especially his mom's, and there was no mistaking what was going on: They were laughing. Nickel knew his mom's laugh anywhere — though he hadn't been hearing it much lately.

There was something about the two of them together laughing that made Nickel uneasy. He would have preferred that they had been arguing. Then at least he could be sure that one of them was defending him. Both of them laughing made him worry that he was the joke.

He tried comforting himself by imagining that they were laughing about something else — that is, something that had absolutely nothing to do with him. Maybe Mr. Kirkaby had told her one of his jokes. Mr. Kirkaby knew a lot of jokes. Maybe he had told her the one about the porcupine and the bubble gum. That was a good one. But then, thinking of his mom and Mr. Kirkaby idly chatting, telling jokes, and being friendly, he suddenly felt more uneasy.

What if they got MARRIED? he thought with horror. *They're both single. They're about the same age, the same height. They're both teachers.*

The idea of it was too awful to imagine. He jumped up out of his seat and began pacing the hall.

"Hey, Nickel!" Scott Pfister said, appearing on the stairs with his mother. "Your mom in there?"

Nickel nodded. He didn't look Scott in the eye. He didn't want Scott to see his desperation.

"Sounds like they're having a good time!" Scott's mother said.

Nickel snorted and returned to his seat. He turned and faced the wall.

When — finally — the door to Nickel's classroom

opened, his mom emerged red-faced and moist-eyed. Mr. Kirkaby was right behind her with an enormous smile on his face.

"Good-bye, Maud," he said. "Always a pleasure."

"Maud"? Nickel thought. What happened to "Ms. Wilde"?

"You, too, Duncan," his mom replied.

DUNCAN!

"Come on, Nickel," she said, putting her arm around his shoulder and leading him away.

"Ready, Ms. Pfister?" Nickel heard Mr. Kirkaby say behind him.

"Ms. Pfister," Nickel thought. But he calls MY mom "Maud"!

"Your teacher is very funny," his mom said, once they'd turned the corner.

Nickel grumbled.

"He thinks the world of you, you know."

Nickel looked up at her. He didn't know.

"He says you pick things up quickly, and that you're creative and intuitive. He also said you're very well-behaved and respectful." She smiled. "You're a little dreamy sometimes, he says — off in your own world — and you don't mix much with the other kids, but that that's nothing to fret about. Galileo was solitary and dreamy, too, and he turned out all right."

"Galileo was tried as a heretic and confined to his home for the rest of his life," Nickel said sourly.

His mom laughed and rubbed his head. "You know what I mean."

"I'm hungry," Nickel said, wanting to change the subject.

"Well, we'll have to grab something quick," his mom said, checking her watch.

They ran into Angelo's on their way downtown. Nickel looked for the two girls his mom had photographed leaning against the building but they weren't there. Neither was the man with the sea captain's hat. He didn't really think they would be. Nickel ordered a slice with mushrooms, his mom, a slice with black olives, and they rushed down the sidewalk, eating as they went.

"Did you ever feel like you're a mouse in a maze?" his mom said as they turned the corner.

"What do you mean?"

"The city," his mom said, waving her arm. "It's like a maze — a concrete maze — and we just scurry along, trying to find our way."

"Our way to what?"

"Good question!"

"To where ends meet?" Nickel asked.

His mom laughed to herself. "Maybe," she said.

They caught the 33 inbound bus at 20th Street and De-Witt and took it all the way to 2nd. They turned the corner and there was the Kalamata Café.

"Okay," his mom said, looking around. "Which way from here?"

Nickel stared up at her. He had been counting on her remembering.

"You don't know?" his mom asked a little frantically.

Nickel shook his head.

"How did you find it before?"

"Inez," Nickel said. "She found it on the map."

He pointed at the map in the bus stop beside them, the one where the woman with the Pekingese had been. His mom rushed over to it.

"Here's where we are," she said, pointing at the YOU ARE HERE arrow. "There's a dead end alley right around the corner of that block." She pointed across the street. "Come on!" She grabbed Nickel's hand and raced for the corner.

Nickel stumbled along behind her the best he could. His mom's legs were longer and made ground much quicker. He glanced up at the sky and saw a marmoset, standing on its head. And then he saw a puffer fish, puffed up. Then a sheep. And another sheep. So many sheep.

"Here!" his mom said suddenly. She stopped.

Nickel looked down. They were at the alley.

11

THE door to the Beastly Arms was no longer gray. It had been painted blue. Sky blue. It opened moments after Nickel's mom rang the bell. In the doorway stood a man wearing a suit of clothes — brown with flecks of black and white in it — and a brown bow tie and brown-and-white saddle shoes, freshly polished.

"Good afternoon!" he said cheerfully, his big, dark eyes gleaming. He extended his hand to Nickel's mom. "Julius Beastly. Pleased to meet you."

Nickel closed his eyes and opened them again. It was Mr. Beastly all right. He wouldn't have guessed in a million years.

His mom seemed equally surprised. She hid it with a smile. "Maud Wilde," she said, taking his hand and shaking it.

Mr. Beastly bowed forward slightly. "Charmed," he said. He looked down at Nickel. "Good to see you again, Nicholas. Where's your friend?"

Nickel almost said "Inez?" but then realized who Mr. Beastly meant. He opened his pocket and Miriam peeked out.

Mr. Beastly smiled. "So glad you could come, Miriam!" He reached out his hand and Miriam jumped into it. "Such a friendly creature!" Mr. Beastly said. Miriam hopped up his coat sleeve to his shoulder.

"My son says you have an apartment for rent," Nickel's mom said.

"Yes," Mr. Beastly said, scooping Miriam off his shoulder and handing her back to Nickel. "Please, come inside." He stepped backward and, again, bowed slightly.

"Thank you," Nickel's mom said, stepping past him into the building.

Nickel followed behind her, smiling at Mr. Beastly as he passed. He couldn't get over the change. Everything was different: his expression, his posture, his attitude, his clothes. He'd combed his hair and had even shaved off his beard. As they walked toward the lobby, Nickel glanced back over his shoulder and caught Mr. Beastly yawning a great yawn. He noticed that his eyes still had circles under them. He was still tired.

"Oh!" his mom said from the lobby. "It's beautiful!"

When Nickel entered the room, he saw that, like the front door — and Mr. Beastly — it looked renewed. The walls were freshly painted a cheery yellow. Lush vining plants in huge ceramic pots hung on ropes from the high ceiling, filtering the light from the skylight and creating dappled shadows on the wall. The floor was covered by a sprawling woolen rug with shapes of animals woven into it: a lion, a snake, a brightly colored bird with flowing plumage — a quetzal, Nickel guessed. On the rug sat the same wooden table and chairs, only now painted red. The cobwebs were gone.

"How on earth do you water?" his mom asked, leaning her head back as far as it would go.

"With this!" Mr. Beastly said proudly. He disappeared into the vines. "This way!" he called out through them.

Nickel's mom cautiously parted the vines to reveal Mr. Beastly standing in the corner of the room beside a very tall ladder.

"You see?" he said, smiling.

Nickel's mom nodded then released the vines. She leaned over to Nickel and whispered, "Is he crazy?"

Nickel shook his head.

"Please," Mr. Beastly said, reappearing through the tangle. He gestured for Nickel and his mom to sit, and they all took a seat around the table. Mr. Beastly's face suddenly grew very serious.

"I want to apologize for before, Mrs. Wilde," he said.

"Ms.," Nickel's mom said.

Mr. Beastly looked confused. "I beg your pardon?"

"Ms." Nickel's mom said again. "Ms. Wilde. Not Mrs."

Mr. Beastly still looked confused. "Miss?"

Nickel's mom shook her head. "Never mind. Call me Maud."

Mr. Beastly smiled. "Thank you," he said. "And, please, call me Julius." His face grew serious again. "Now, I wanted to explain about before, about the other day. I was not myself. I had some sort of . . . thing. A bug of some kind."

Nickel's mom leaned back away from him.

"Oh, it's gone!" Mr. Beastly insisted. "It was probably one of those twenty-four-hour things! I feel fine now!" He pounded his fist against his chest, which caused him to cough.

"I see," Nickel's mom said. She gave Nickel a look out of the corner of her eyes.

"Would you like to see the apartment?" Mr. Beastly asked, standing up.

"Please," Nickel's mom said.

Mr. Beastly led them up the staircase in the corner, the one that had disappeared into darkness before but that now was well-lit and carpeted. Nickel tilted his head back and saw the staircase spiraling up at least four or five more flights.

"What's that?" Nickel's mom said when they reached the landing. She sniffed the air.

Mr. Beastly sniffed at the lapel of his jacket. "I apologize," he said, his face reddening. "It must be this old jacket. I must admit I haven't worn it in a while. It's been in a cedar chest to keep the moths away. I just had an impulse today to get it out and see if it still fits. What do you think?" He spun around.

"Fine," Nickel's mom said, forcing a grin. Then, behind Mr. Beastly's back, she tugged at Nickel's shirtsleeve and spun her finger around her ear.

The floor creaked as they followed Mr. Beastly down the hall. The white walls smelled of fresh paint. There were apartment doors every few feet on either side — 2A, 2B, 2C, 2D. Potted plants on pedestals stood in between. The only window was at the far end of the hall. It was shuttered.

Mr. Beastly stopped in front of 2E. It was the third door on the left.

"Here we are!" he said. He turned the knob and pushed the door open. "After you, please."

"Thank you," Nickel's mom said.

They entered into a small foyer. A narrow hall led off to the left. To the right was a closed door, which Nickel presumed to be a coat closet. Straight ahead was a big empty living room. It was square and tall with hardwood floors, newly polished. Floor-to-ceiling bookshelves had been built into the two side walls. On the opposite wall were three tall windows, side by side. Out the windows there was a red-brick wall. The light bouncing off of it cast the room in soft red light.

"Nice," Nickel's mom cooed.

"The bedrooms are this way," Mr. Beastly said, leading them down the hall.

The first door they came to opened into one of the bedrooms. It was long and narrow and had one tall window at the end with the same view as the living room's. Nickel went over to it, pulled it open, and poked his head outside. Below was a long narrow gap between the Beastly Arms and the red-brick building next door. The bottom of it was clogged with weeds and bushes. It ended to the left with another red-brick wall. To the right, it appeared to open into a bigger space behind the Beastly Arms.

The second door led into a bathroom. It had a claw-foot bathtub, a shell-shaped sink, and a small separate room just for the toilet. There was no window.

"This door connects to the master bedroom," Mr. Beastly said, opening a door beside the sink. Nickel's mom stepped through it.

"*Very* nice!" she said.

The room was twice as wide as the first bedroom. It had two tall windows, side by side, with the same view of the bricks. Against the far wall of the apartment was a king-size four-poster bed, made up with pillows and a down comforter.

"The bed was left behind by a former occupant," Mr. Beastly said when he saw Nickel's mom eyeing it. "I laundered all the linens. If it's inconvenient, I can have it taken out."

"Inconvenient!" Nickel's mom sighed, running her fingers over the comforter. "I've always *dreamed* of a bed like this!"

Mr. Beastly smiled. "Well, then," he said. "We'll leave it. Would you like to see the kitchen?"

Nickel's mom nodded, and they followed Mr. Beastly back down the hall and through the living room, into the kitchen. It was four or five times the size of their kitchen at the Gardenview. The counters were deep and long with lots of wooden cabinets underneath and above. There was an old gas stove, a small fridge, and a large kitchen table with four chairs. There was one window. It had the same view as all the other rooms (red bricks) and the same rosy glow.

"Again," Mr. Beastly said, "the table doesn't have to stay. I'm sure you have your own table."

Nickel giggled, and his mom shot him a look.

"Okay," she said to Mr. Beastly. "It's beautiful. Wonderful. For this city, a palace! But I'm afraid there's no way we can afford it. I didn't mean to take up your time. I had no idea it was this nice. Nickel must have made a mistake. You see," she rolled her eyes, "he told me the rent was two hundred dollars. I assumed he heard wrong. What do kids know about money, right? But, I thought, well, I'll check it out. I figured it would be a dive. But obviously Nickel did make a mistake. What is it? Two thousand? Two thousand two hundred?"

"It's two hundred," Mr. Beastly said, smiling. "A month."

Nickel's mom blinked at him a couple of times. Then she took a breath, let it out and said, "Look, I don't know what's going on here. Maybe I'm slow. Maybe you're crazy. If you're saying you're renting this apartment for two hundred dollars a month, my bet is the latter!"

Mr. Beastly still smiled. "I may be crazy, Maud," he said, "but two hundred is all I'm asking. Two hundred is all I need. Look where we are. Look at this neighborhood. If I charge more, I don't get paid. Then I have problems. I see that you are a responsible person, hard-working, a good parent. I trust you. So I say two hundred because I figure you could use a break, because I know you'll pay your rent. I know you'll take care of my apartment, of my bed."

"Your bed?" Nickel's mom asked.

"I mean the bed," Mr. Beastly said quickly. "Two hundred is reasonable. It is fair. And your presence in this neighborhood would most certainly be an improvement. If the rent makes life easier for you, then more the better."

Nickel's mom leaned back against the counter. "I don't know," she said. "I don't even know why I came here. His father would probably sue for custody if I moved into this neighborhood. Not that he's doing anything to prevent it from happening." She brought her hand up to her forehead.

Mr. Beastly pulled a folded set of papers out of the inside pocket of his jacket. "This is the lease," he said. "Take it with you. Read it over. There's no rush." He held it out to her. "Think about it."

She looked at it for a second as if it might bite her, then took it. "Okay," she said. "I'll think about it."

Nickel wished his mom would just say yes. He knew she'd take the lease home and read it over thoroughly and sleep on it, and then discuss it with his dad — not that she'd listen to what he'd have to say. But Nickel wished she'd just sign it, right then and there. He wanted to live in the Beastly Arms, even if it meant leaving his old neighborhood, his school, the park, Inez. At that moment he didn't care. He didn't really know why, but he wanted to live in the Beastly Arms more than anything in the world. He could feel it in his bones. In his belly. He wanted his mom to sign the lease.

"We couldn't move in for thirty days," she said suddenly. "We'd have to give notice."

Nickel gaped at her.

"Fine," Mr. Beastly said. "I'll hold it for you."

"Can I leave you a deposit?" Nickel's mom asked.

"Not necessary," Mr. Beastly said. "Have we got a deal?" He took a pen out of his vest and held it out to her.

Nickel's mom looked over at Nickel. He nodded as hard as he could.

"On one condition," she said. "I pay you three hundred dollars a month, and not a penny less. Change it on the lease and I'll sign it."

Mr. Beastly smiled. "You drive a hard bargain, Maud," he said.

He took the lease from her, changed the two to a three, and handed it back to her, along with the pen. She set the lease on the counter and signed it.

Mr. Beastly held out his hand. Nickel's mom shook it. Then Mr. Beastly shook Nickel's hand and Miriam's paw.

"Welcome to the Beastly Arms!" he said.

12

FOR the first time, Nickel walked back down the alley without being dragged. He thought about how many times in the future he would walk down it: leaving home for school, for the library, for the darkroom. It would become like Ira Monk Street, as much a part of where he lived as the room in which he slept. He wanted to know its name, but could find no signs.

Across the street he saw the bright yellow storefront of a check-cashing place. The red neon sign in the window kept flashing CASH! over and over. All of its windows had iron bars. Beside the check-cashing place was a Vietnamese market. The white canvas awning over the door was covered with words that Nickel couldn't read, but could recognize as Vietnamese. The market's windows weren't barred; instead, there was one of those big metal grates that covered the whole storefront and could be rolled up during business hours and rolled down at night. Next to the market was a brick storefront, painted black, with no windows at all. The words "The Oasis" were written in red cursive neon on a sign jutting out over the sidewalk. Nickel knew that such places were bars.

Of the three landmarks, the Oasis was the most distinctive. There were check-cashing places and Vietnamese markets all over downtown, but only one black Oasis. He would try to remember it, should he have trouble finding his way back again.

"Well," his mom sighed. Nickel had almost forgotten she was there. "I didn't expect *that* to happen!"

Nickel looked up at her and saw that she was staring straight ahead. He could tell that she wasn't looking at anything. Her eyes were turned inward.

"Do you know what the name of the street is?" he asked.

"What?" she said, snapping out of her thoughts. "The street?"

"The alley. What's our new address?"

"I don't know," his mom said. She unfolded her copy of the lease. "Let's see . . . it's One Tall Grass Drive, apartment 2E."

"Tall Grass?" Nickel said.

His mom laughed. "Must have been named a long time ago!"

Nickel tried to imagine the cement underfoot covered in tall grass, and then said, "Look!" At his feet, etched permanently into the pavement, were the words TALL GRASS DR.

"That's Ira Monk Street, you know," his mom said, pointing out at the busy street ahead of them. "The Gardenview is just sixteen blocks up that way." She pointed off to the right.

Ira Monk Street? Nickel thought. He couldn't believe it! It didn't seem possible that this could be the same street that he lived on! Only sixteen blocks away and it was like another world!

"I hope I did the right thing," his mom said. "This really isn't the best neighborhood. But the building is beautiful, don't you think? And that apartment! That *bed!* *Oh!*"

Nickel wondered if he should tell her how different everything had been before, how on Saturday everything had been been so drab, including Mr. Beastly. Surely the building didn't have a twenty-four hour bug. Obviously, Mr. Beastly had had the place painted and decorated since then, or done it himself.

"I'll talk to Mr. Youdle tonight," his mom said. "And then I guess I'll call your dad. I can just imagine what he's going to say!" She rolled her eyes.

Nickel felt a raindrop on his nose, then on his arm. His mom must have felt one, too, for she held out her palms and looked up.

"We'd better get going," she said, opening her umbrella.

They quickly walked past the Kalamata Café to the bus stop. Nickel's mom put him on the Number 46 outbound bus and headed off toward the subway. Nickel watched her red umbrella through the bus's window until it was eclipsed by a street sign.

He didn't get off at 17th street and go home; he stayed on until 18th and then ran through the rain the few blocks to the library. He zoomed past the concrete lions into the building, shook off the rain in the vestibule, then walked past the circulation desk into the central hall. He looked up at the dome. Without the sun, he couldn't see the dust.

"Earth to Nickel," a voice whispered from behind him. "Earth to Nickel. Come in, Space Cadet Dill."

Nickel spun around. It was Inez! He was so glad to see her!

"My mom signed the lease!" he gushed. "We're moving to the Beastly Arms!"

"Huh?" Inez said, flummoxed.

He told her how different the place had looked, how it had rugs and paint and plants now, and how different Mr. Beastly had been, how he'd said he'd been sick before — which was why he'd been so strange. He described the apartment and how much his mom loved it, and then he told her again how she'd signed the lease and how they would be moving there in only a month. Only a month! His voice got louder and louder as he went on.

"That's great," Inez said without sounding like she meant it one bit. She folded her arms across her chest.

Nickel felt all his excitement drain out of his body onto the cold marble floor. "What's wrong?" he asked.

"Nothing," Inez said. "Everything's perfect." Again, the tone of her voice sounded just the opposite of her words. "How did your mom's conference go with Mr. Kirkaby?" She was changing the subject.

"Okay," Nickel sighed. His shoulders slumped. *Why did she have to bring THAT up?*

"Ms. Cardenal told my mom I was exceptional," Inez said with her eyes closed and her chin raised.

"Aren't you glad for me?" Nickel asked.

"Glad?" Inez said, pretending to be confused. "Why, of course I'm glad! I couldn't be happier!" Her voice wasn't happy.

Suddenly, Nickel understood. Why had he thought Inez would be glad that he would be moving downtown? She wasn't even *allowed* downtown. They'd see each other much less — if at all. He might even have to go to a different school. The idea of that didn't make him happy, either. But all he'd been able to think about was his new room, his new building, his new landlord, and maybe, for once, making ends meet. And then, of course, there was also the secret. Surely living right inside the Beastly Arms would help him to discover it. He hadn't given any thought to Inez's feelings at all. He assumed that if he was happy, she'd be, too, the way his dad always assumed Nickel would be happy shopping or golfing or going to the zoo.

"We can still do stuff together," he said softly.

"Of course we can," she said. She was still being sarcastic.

"I can come to your house," Nickel said. "We can come here."

Inez shrugged and glanced away.

"We can talk on the phone," Nickel said.

Inez peered up at the dome. "Out of sight, out of mind," she said liltingly.

"Huh?" Nickel said.

"Out of sight, out of mind," Inez said again. She slowly rolled her eyes back down. "Don't you know what that means?"

"You won't be out of mind," Nickel said.

"We won't see each other at recess anymore!" she said loudly. "Or at lunch! We won't walk home together! *Out of sight, out of mind!*"

"Ssssh!" hissed a woman sitting at a desk across the room.

Inez turned and glowered at her.

"I don't know," Nickel whispered. "I'll probably still go to the same school. Mom won't want me to change. She likes Mr. Kirkaby." He felt a pang in his stomach at the thought.

"*Probably* isn't getting it!" Inez said, moving her shoulders up and down, one after the other, as she spoke. It was an expression and a gesture that her mother often used.

"I'll ask Mom tonight," Nickel said. "Then I'll call you."

Inez shrugged and looked away. "Suit yourself," she said. This was also Ms. Willamina.

"What's that you're reading?" Nickel asked, noticing she had a book tucked under her arm.

Inez held it up. It was called *Albania*.

"Oh," Nickel said. "So you're going to interview Mrs. Bislimi?"

"Uh-huh," Inez said. "I wanted to read up a little first."

"That's a good idea," Nickel said. He wondered what he could read to help him with Mr. Beastly.

"Who are you going to interview?" Inez asked.

Nickel thought it best to avoid any mention of anything having to do with Mr. Beastly or where he lived for the time being. But before he could answer, Inez said, "Mr. Beastly, I bet."

There was no hiding anything from her.

"Did you find out the secret yet?" she asked.

Nickel shook his head.

"You will," she said. "Especially now. If you're any kind of a detective at all, you'll find it out real quick."

"I'm not a detective," Nickel said. "I'm a photographer."

"All detectives use cameras. Don't you watch TV?"

Nickel didn't need to answer. She knew he didn't. He and his mom didn't even own one. His mom called TV "a waste of time for anyone with any imagination." Anyway, they didn't have one.

"Well, come on," Inez said. "Let's find some books on detecting."

At last she smiled. Nickel heaved a sigh of relief, and then let her drag him into the children's book room by his shirtsleeve.

"You can probably keep going to the same school," Nickel's mom answered. "I'll go in with you tomorrow and we'll ask Duncan."

"Duncan," Nickel thought. *She'll ask "Duncan."*

While his mom prepared dinner. Nickel sat on his bed in his room reading a book about detecting. It explained how to fix a door so that you can tell if someone had opened it. It could be a regular door, a cabinet, or even a refrigerator door. The trick also worked on drawers, windows, and purses. The book also explained how to dust for fingerprints, how to follow someone without being seen, how to tell if someone is telling the truth by watching their eyes and hands, how to pick locks, how to tap phones, and how to understand the criminal mind.

Nickel wasn't so sure he'd be willing to do any of these things, nor whether, if he was willing, they would help him to uncover Mr. Beastly's secret. He had a hunch, actually, that uncovering the secret wouldn't take much effort anyway. He had a feeling that Mr. Beastly actually *wanted* to reveal it to him. That was why he'd had everything painted and why he'd gotten all dressed up.

He wants us to live there, Nickel thought. *He wants us to because he wants to tell me his secret. Nobody likes keeping secrets. Secrets are always whining to get out. Like dogs.*

When Nickel closed his book and looked up, he saw that it was the golden hour. On the ceiling, his cloud photographs were bathed in golden light just as they had been when he had taken them.

He climbed down from his bed and went to the window. He leaned his head out and gazed up at the sky. It was filled with golden-edged clouds. He saw a raccoon chasing its ringed tail, which brought back the image of the raccoon in the street near the Beastly Arms. The memory was so strong that it blocked out the sky.

Suddenly, Nickel was struck with an idea. He got a notebook and pencil from his desk, then returned to the window. He looked back up at the raccoon cloud, studied its shape, then closed his eyes. He could still see it in his mind's eye. When he reopened his eyes, he held the notebook up to his face and a ghost of the raccoon cloud appeared on it.

"Persistence of vision," he said to himself.

He quickly traced its outline with his pencil. When he was done, he held the notebook at an arm's distance to see how it looked. It looked like a raccoon.

He flipped the page and leaned out the window again. He saw a moth with a bite taken out of its wing. *A bat must have gotten to it,* he thought with a grin. He closed his eyes. The moth cloud floated across the inside of his eyelids. When he opened them again, he traced it in his notebook. Then he repeated the process again, over and over, his eyes opening and shutting like a shutter, his retinas holding the images, like film.

He showed his mom his pictures after dinner on the

couch. She smiled and said, "Clouds shouldn't be ruled. I'll get you a sketchbook."

Later that night in his room, he heard his mom through the wall talking to his dad on the phone in her room. His dad's voice was so loud on the phone that it sounded as if he were in there with her.

Nickel stood up on his bed and took down the photographs from the ceiling. He replaced them with his drawings, then lay on his bed, looking up at them and waiting for his mom to hang up the phone so he could call Inez and tell her "probably."

Nickel and his mom arrived early at his school the next morning so that she could talk to Mr. Kirkaby — Duncan — and still make her eight-thirty class. Mr. Kirkaby led them to the principal's office. Ms. Stonecipher told Nickel's mom to fill out a few forms and submit them to the district office, but that, probably, Nickel would be allowed to finish out the school year there. Probably. In the fall he'd be going into middle school, and he would be placed in the one nearest his new home.

Nickel's mom thanked her, picked up the forms from the secretary, thanked Mr. Kirkaby — "Thanks for all your help, Duncan" — then rushed off to work.

"Do you like the apartment you'll be moving into?" Mr. Kirkaby asked.

Nickel nodded.

"Do you and your mom need any help?"

Nickel had to think about this. Would his dad help? He probably would, provided his mom asked him. But she probably wouldn't ask. She'd probably prefer for them to do it alone than to have to listen to his dad complain all day about the building and the neighborhood and all. She might ask some of her friends at work, though. And she'd ask Inez's parents to help. They often helped her out with things like this. He hoped she'd ask them. Mr. Willamina always made things fun. Maybe Inez would come along. Maybe she'd help Nickel do some detecting.

"Well," Mr. Kirkaby said, "tell her that if she needs an extra back I'd be happy to drop by."

Nickel looked up at him, bewildered. Was his teacher really offering to come over — *to his house?* Again the sickening thought of Mr. Kirkaby and his mom marrying crossed his mind.

"We have plenty of help," Nickel said.

"Well, good," Mr. Kirkaby said with a slight smile. "I imagine someone like your mother has lots of friends."

"*Someone like my mom?*" Nickel thought. *What does THAT mean? What was his mom like that she'd have lots of friends? Was that some kind of a compliment or something?*

Nickel stopped when they passed the library, saying he had homework to finish. The truth was that there was still a half hour before the bell rang and Nickel didn't want to spend it sitting in the classroom with Duncan.

"Need a little more time to think, huh?" Mr. Kirkaby said, grinning.

Nickel looked up at him, bewildered again.

"That was your homework, Nickel," Mr. Kirkaby said. "To think."

"Oh, I already did that," Nickel said. "But I still have math to do from last week."

Mr. Kirkaby smiled. "Right," he said. "I'll see you in class."

Nickel did his math in the library then sat and read a book about bats until the bell rang. Inez was waiting for him in the hall outside his classroom.

"Well?" she said.

Nickel told her that Ms. Stonecipher said he'd probably be able to stay.

"*Probably* isn't getting it!" Inez said, folding her arms in front of her.

Nickel rolled his eyes.

The last bell rang seconds after Nickel took his seat. The class listened to Ms. Stonecipher's announcements, then Mr. Kirkaby took roll from his desk.

"Another day on Earth," he said, stepping in front of the class. "Let's make the most of it."

That day this meant learning a new math concept: a decimal repeating to infinity. Mr. Kirkaby showed them how one-third equaled .333333333333333 . . . — and on and on like that forever. *An infinity of threes,* Nickel thought. He couldn't imagine it. Then they started a new section in social studies: South America. After recess, Mr.

Kirkaby asked everyone to write down the names of the people they were planning to interview — their subjects, he called them — and any information they already knew about them.

Nickel wrote his name and the date at the top of a sheet of notebook paper. He wrote MY INTERVIEW SUBJECT on the top line, centered, as Mr. Kirkaby had instructed. Then he dropped down a few lines and began:

I am going to interview Julius Beastly. He is an old man that lives downtown in the Beastly Arms Apartments. It's on Tall Grass Drive. Sometimes he's very nice. Sometimes he's kind of weird. He has a very tall ladder. He was sick on Saturday. He has a secret and I want to know what it is.

He stopped and read back what he'd written. It seemed short. He tried to think of other things that he knew about Mr. Beastly. He closed his eyes and saw him in the door-way, in his robe, then in his suit. He saw him in the drab, empty lobby and in the painted one with all the hanging plants. He saw him in the kitchen in apartment 2E, shaking Miriam's paw. Then he added:

He knows a lot about kangaroo rats.

PART TWO

IN
THE
BEASTLY
ARMS

13

OVER the next couple weeks, Nickel used up three fifty-page sketchbooks and started a fourth. His ceiling was plastered with unlined drawings of clouds. His camera remained in his drawer, unloaded, with his filters, his lens tissue, and his underwear.

His class finished Brazil, Bolivia, Venezuela, Colombia, Ecuador, and Peru. They moved on from decimals going off to infinity to irrational numbers. They also had selected their interview subjects and drafted their interview questions. All that was left to do was to go out, conduct the interviews, and write them up.

The proper procedure for requesting and conducting an interview, according to Mr. Kirkaby, was to call ahead and request a time convenient for the subject, then show up promptly at that time prepared with questions, paper, several sharpened pencils, and a tape recorder with several blank tapes. Tape recorders were available for check out in the Media Center.

"Be neatly dressed, polite, and to the point," Mr.

Kirkaby told the class. "Don't waste the subject's time going off on wild tangents. Listen more than talk. The subject, on the other hand, should be encouraged to ramble. Rambling can reveal a lot about a person. When the arranged time for ending the interview comes, politely dismiss yourself, thanking the subject and offering to deliver a copy of the interview when it is finished. Then, as quickly as possible, sit down somewhere and review your notes and tapes. It's important to organize this information while the interview is still fresh in your mind. If you find you did not collect all the information you need, call and arrange for a brief follow-up interview, apologizing for the inconvenience."

Nickel stumbled over the first hurdle: He couldn't call ahead. Mr. Beastly didn't have a phone. Mr. Kirkaby said it was all right in that case for Nickel to request an interview in person.

Nickel hadn't been back to the Beastly Arms since the day his mom signed the lease, and was glad for a reason to go. He got off the bus at 2nd and Ira Monk, then walked down 2nd until he spotted the black Oasis across the street. For the first time he found the alley himself. He walked through the dusky light to the sky blue door. His bush baby eyes reflected in the brass nameplate. He smoothed down his hair, then rang the bell.

No one answered. He rang again. Still no one. He couldn't decide to ring again or not. What if Mr. Beastly was sleeping and didn't want to be disturbed? He decided to leave, but just as he was turning away, the lock clicked, the knob turned, and the door opened. Nickel turned back, anxious to see Mr. Beastly's smiling face, anxious to be let inside, anxious to see his new home again. But Mr. Beastly wasn't smiling.

"What is it?" he growled, peering around the door, his eyes squinted into slits. "What do you want?"

"It's m-me, Mr. Beastly," Nickel said timidly. "N-Nicholas Dill." He patted his shirt pocket. "And Miriam."

Miriam poked her nose out and sniffed.

Mr. Beastly's scowl loosened. He seemed bewildered, half asleep, not exactly there. Finally, he opened the door a bit more. He was back in his shabby gray robe. His face was covered with an inch of beard.

"Nicholas Dill," Mr. Beastly said, straightening his robe and tightening its belt. "Nicholas. Yes. Good to see you, my boy. Are you folks moving in today? Time must have gotten away from me."

"We're not moving in," Nickel said. "Not for a couple weeks. I just wanted to ask you something."

"Of course, of course," Mr. Beastly said, and gestured for Nickel to enter.

As he walked through the foyer, Nickel looked back over his shoulder and saw Mr. Beastly yawning a great yawn. In the lobby, the leaves of the hanging plants were drooping.

"Are your plants okay?" he asked.

"What's that?" Mr. Beastly said, looking up. "Oh, yes. No. No, they're not. It's my fault. I've just been so busy with — well, I haven't had the time to water as I should."

"Can I help?"

"Oh, no, no," Mr. Beastly said, shaking his head. "It's for me to do. I'm glad you mentioned it, in fact. I keep forgetting. I'll get to it this morning."

Nickel thought that that was a strange thing to say. It was four o'clock in the afternoon.

"Well," Mr. Beastly said, guiding Nickel into a chair at the table and then sitting down beside him. "What is it you wanted to ask?"

Nickel noticed that the table had cobwebs on the legs again.

"I have this assignment at school," he said. "I'm supposed to interview someone. It can't be family or someone I live with."

"You can't interview Miriam then, I guess," Mr. Beastly said, grinning and pointing at Nickel's pocket.

"No," Nickel said seriously. "I was wondering if you'd let me interview *you.*"

Mr. Beastly scratched the top of his head. "*Me?*"

Nickel nodded.

"Now?" Mr. Beastly asked.

"No. I just want to make an appointment now." He thought of Mr. Kirkaby's instructions. "At a time that's convenient for you."

Mr. Beastly stood up and walked back and forth across the rug. Nickel saw that he was barefoot again. His feet were filthy.

"Why not?" Mr. Beastly said suddenly, turning and facing Nickel. "How about tomorrow?"

Nickel smiled. "Sure! What time?"

"How about the same time as now? What time *is* it?"

"About four," Nickel said, then added, "in the afternoon."

"Then tomorrow at four," Mr. Beastly said brightly. "In the afternoon."

"Okay," Nickel said, with a smile.

"Now," Mr. Beastly said, looking around. "Where's that watering can?"

He strode out of the room and returned moments later with a large tin watering can sloshing over with water.

"Better leave Miriam down here with me," he said. "I don't think she'll like it up there." He reached out toward Nickel's shirt pocket and Miriam hopped out into his hand. There was a pumpkin seed waiting for her.

Then he handed the can to Nickel and sent him up the ladder.

Nickel returned the next day at four o'clock sharp. He had his interview questions and one of the school's tape recorders (plus tapes) in his backpack and Miriam in his shirt pocket. Mr. Beastly opened the door before Nickel could ring the bell.

"Right on time!" he said, beaming. He had on his black-and-white-flecked brown suit, his brown bow tie, and his shiny brown-and-white saddle shoes again. He had added a brown felt hat and a wristwatch to the outfit. "A good reporter's always on time," he said, stepping outside and shutting and locking the door behind him. "I suppose you have all your questions ready?"

Nickel looked up at him, dazed. *Why is he coming out?* he wondered. Nickel had imagined the interview taking place inside, at the red wooden table in the lobby. *Where are we going?* he thought as Mr. Beastly walked right past him and headed off down the alley.

"Come on now," Mr. Beastly said over his shoulder. "Your subject's getting away!"

Nickel stood there a second more, then, still confused, ran to catch up.

"I thought we'd stroll while we talked," Mr. Beastly said as he reached Ira Monk Street and turned left. "Fresh air's good for the brain." He took a deep breath and let it out. His face soured. "Well, at least it's *air*," he said with a raised eyebrow.

"My questions are in my bag," Nickel said, struggling to keep up. Mr. Beastly was moving at a brisk pace.

"You don't know them by heart?"

"Uh-uh," Nickel grunted, swinging his backpack around and fumbling with the zipper. Miriam let out a loud chirp, but it was too late. Nickel slammed into a big green mailbox.

He saw stars. For a moment he didn't know where he was or what he was doing. Then Miriam hopped up onto his shoulder and tickled his cheek with her whiskers. Nickel peered around the mailbox and saw Mr. Beastly disappear around the corner onto 1st Street. "A good reporter thinks on his feet," he was saying up ahead. Nickel jumped to his feet and ran down the sidewalk, the tape recorder in his backpack banging against his spine.

When he turned the corner he nearly collided with a man pushing a small shopping cart. "Watch where you're going!" the man shouted as Nickel weaved around him and promptly tripped over the man's dog, which was trailing behind on a leash. The dog began snarling and barking and baring its teeth. Miriam hunkered down in Nickel's pocket. Nickel tried to get to his feet but was entangled in the leash.

"He'll bite you if you keep messing with him!" the man said.

The dog's teeth looked sharp. Nickel reached down and unwound the leash from his leg. The man and his dog turned around the corner. Mr. Beastly was nowhere in sight.

"Mr. Beastly!" Nickel called out.

He ran down 1st Street toward Ivy. On the corner he looked frantically in every direction. Then, up ahead and across the street, he caught a glimpse of Mr. Beastly backing out of a building's entryway. His head was tilted back, and he was looking up at the building towering over him.

"Mr. Beastly!" Nickel yelled again. He ran into Ivy Street. The light was flashing DON'T WALK. Car horns blared. People hollered. Nickel closed his eyes and ran on. At the curb, he opened them and looked back to where Mr. Beastly had been. He was gone.

Nickel ran back across 1st Street without checking for traffic. The light was flashing DON'T WALK again. Again there was honking and yelling. When he reached the other side, someone tapped him on the shoulder from behind.

"Reporting's dangerous work," a voice said.

Nickel spun around. It was Mr. Beastly.

"You should be more careful," he said. "Don't you know yet about crossing signals? 'Look to the left, look to the right. Cross at the corner, cross at the light.'" He smiled down at Nickel.

Nickel didn't answer. He leaned forward, his hands on his knees, and tried to catch his breath.

"You see that one there?" Mr. Beastly said. "That's one of mine."

Nickel twisted his head to see what Mr. Beastly was talking about. He was pointing at a building across the street — an old theater, with a box office, a marquee, and a sign that ran up the corner edge of the building two or three floors. The sign was lined with small clear light-bulbs, many of them missing or broken. It read, vertically, "Rialto," with the R at the top and the O at the bottom. All of the doors and windows on the first floor were boarded up and littered with graffiti.

"1933," Mr. Beastly said. "It's been shuttered up for years. It was a church for a while, ten years ago or so. Southern Baptist, I think." He stared at the building, his hands clasped in front of him, as if he were looking upon a loved one's gravestone.

Nickel straightened up. "How old are you?" he asked suddenly. It was the first question on his list.

"I'm older than the Rialto Theater," Mr. Beastly said, looking up. "But younger than the sky." He smiled.

Nickel looked up at the sky with him. It was cloudy and gray. Nickel saw a vampire bat, sneaking up on a horse's foot.

"There's a bat," Mr. Beastly said, pointing up at the clouds. "You see it?"

Nickel nodded. "It's a vampire bat," he said, "sneaking up on a horse."

"So it is!" Mr. Beastly said, laughing. Then he looked down at Nickel. "Well? Next question!"

"Do you own that building?" Nickel asked, pointing at the Rialto. It was not one of his prepared questions.

"Own?" Mr. Beastly said, rubbing his chin. "No, I don't own it. At least not in the way that most people think of owning. I don't have a piece of paper that says it's mine." He looked down at Nickel's shirt pocket. "Do you own *her*?"

Nickel looked down at Miriam. He hadn't ever really thought about it. Sometimes he said "my kangaroo rat" or "my pet, Miriam," but that didn't necessarily mean Miriam was his — a belonging, a possession — any more than his mom or his teacher or his friend, Inez, were.

"Of course not," Mr. Beastly said. "No, if anything, the Rialto owns *me*. When you're responsible for something, or someone, they require your attention, your care. Maybe they don't own you, exactly, but they rely on you. They trust you to do what's right. Like Miriam there. She's not yours. You're hers. She needs you."

Nickel tried to understand all this, but he couldn't keep it straight in his mind. He wished he could hear it all again, and then he remembered the tape recorder. He quickly pulled it out of his backpack and aimed the microphone up at Mr. Beastly.

"What have you got there?" Mr. Beastly said, looking down at the mike. "Oh, you don't need *that*! You'll remember what I say! Good reporters don't need gadgets and gizmos. They just need ears!"

Nickel looked at the black plastic box in his hands. *A camera for sound*, he thought. He shut it off and put it back into his pack.

"Were you a reporter?" Nickel asked. Another question not on the list.

Mr. Beastly laughed. "Come on, my boy." He turned and walked away. Nickel followed closely behind.

"That's one of mine, too," Mr. Beastly said, pointing at a tall old apartment building across the street. "And that one." He pointed at the building beside it. "They're all mine. Or rather, they all own me."

"What about the Beastly Arms?" Nickel asked.

Mr. Beastly stopped walking. A bemused look came over his face. "Oh, yes," he said. "The Beastly Arms owns me, all right. She owns me most of all."

They walked in silence a while after that. Nickel could think of nothing to ask. He couldn't remember any more of the questions on the list. They turned left at the corner. Mr. Beastly stopped once to feed a sparrow sitting on a concrete windowsill with some seed he produced from his jacket pocket, and another time to point out another building that owned him. At 5th Street, they turned left again. Then, at last, Mr. Beastly spoke.

"This city has changed so much," he said, shaking his head. "These sidewalks used to teem with people. But there used to be places to go then. Restaurants and theaters and markets. That used to be Noonan's Bakery." He pointed at an abandoned storefront with iron bars in the front windows. "That was a cobbler's shop." He pointed at a liquor store. "Kids used to play all over around here.

Hopscotch. Jump rope. Four-square. They pitched pennies against the walls.

"But then they widened the streets to let more cars through, and that meant shrinking the sidewalks. You can't stop in a shop when you're in a car, you know. Who could find a place to park? The traffic started backing up, so they widened the road some more. Pedestrians became pests — something to be kept up on the curb. Shops started closing. Not enough foot traffic. The sidewalks became deserted, unsafe. There were muggings, purse snatchings, sometimes shootings. Now they call it a bad neighborhood." He sighed.

"But it used to work," he said. "A city can be like a beehive: crowded, noisy, close, but smooth-running. Sometimes I think it's the best way for people to live — in close quarters, nose to nose. Big city or small town, people seem more human when they know their neighbors. When they know their trees. At least when they're all together, they're not spreading out all over the place, digging more holes and leveling more fields and destroying the livelihood of the world's other animals."

Suddenly, he laughed and slapped Nickel on the shoulder. "Listen to me! 'The good ole days'!" He laughed again. "What an old codger I am!"

At Ira Monk Street, they turned left. They were making a rectangle.

"And how old are you?" Mr. Beastly asked suddenly.

Nickel wanted to answer as cleverly as he had, but could only think of the truth. "Eleven," he said.

"A good age," Mr. Beastly said. "Have you lived in the city all your life?"

"Uh-huh."

"You've never lived in the country? Never in your life?" He seemed disapproving. "Oh, that's a crime! A real crime! One must *choose* to live in the city! One must know what one is giving up!" He made a stern face as he spoke. "You've *been* to the country, of course."

Nickel shook his head again. His mom had no car and no money and his dad, no interest. "I've been golfing," he said, "with my dad."

"*Golfing?*" Mr. Beastly said, horrified. "Golf has nothing

whatsoever to do with nature! Golf has everything to do with man's crazed obsession with order! Order and leisure activities!" He was speaking quite loudly, and when he realized it, he smiled and calmed down.

"Nature likes a mess," he said gently. "Forests and jungles and prairies — they're messy. Or they look that way to us, anyway. But everything in nature has a purpose. Everything gets used. There's muck and scat and rot and filth, and it's gloppy and oozy and squishy and smelly, but it works. It's all necessary. Here, we put what we don't need into big trucks and haul it away where we don't have to look at it. Waste, we call it. It just sits out in the sun not doing anyone any good. That's order for you. That's *civilization* for you! We're always thinking we know better, always thinking we're better than dumb animals."

Nickel thought about this. He thought about how insulted people felt when they were compared to animals. And he thought about how, except for birds and rats and bugs — and pets — there were no animals in the city. That made him think about the raccoon he'd seen with

Inez, the one lying dead in the gutter at the end of Tall Grass Drive. He looked up at Mr. Beastly, who was looking up at the sky as he walked along.

"Why do you live in the city?" he asked him.

Mr. Beastly stopped in his tracks. Suddenly, Nickel realized where they were: They were standing right where the raccoon had been, right at the entrance to the alley. The raccoon was gone. Nickel wondered if it had been hauled away in a truck. Mr. Beastly raised his arm and gestured at the Beastly Arms Apartments at the end of the alley.

"Why do I live here?" he said with a laugh. "Because she needs me! I can't leave her. It wouldn't be right!" Then he bent over and leaned in close to Nickel's ear. "Listen, if ever something in your gut tells you not to do something, don't you do it, even if it's something you've always done. If it seems stupid and wrong all of a sudden, just stop. It's okay. Stop. You see, your gut is nature talking. Listen to it. Otherwise you might end up with something you never really asked for but can't get rid of, no matter what you do."

Nickel wasn't exactly sure what Mr. Beastly was talking

about, but was now positive that he had been right about one thing: Mr. Beastly had a secret. He wasn't so sure anymore, however, how anxious Mr. Beastly was to reveal it.

"I'm tired," Mr. Beastly said, straightening up. He stretched and yawned a great yawn. "Why don't you run along home now. This interview is concluded."

"But I didn't ask you all of the questions I was supposed to!" Nickel whined. He pulled off his bag and began tugging the zipper open.

"Take another look at those questions," Mr. Beastly said. He turned and walked away toward the sky blue door. "I bet I answered them all."

"Can I come back and interview you some more tomorrow?" Nickel begged.

Mr. Beastly stopped and peeked back over his shoulder. "A good reporter takes what he gets," he said. Then he took out his key and let himself into the Beastly Arms.

14

NICKEL knew his way back home well enough now — take Ira Monk Street all the way — that he did not have to rely so much on his mind, leaving it free to pore over Mr. Beastly's words. Nickel did not want to forget them before he could get home and write them down. On the bus, while his eyes checked the street signs going by the windows, his mind replayed his walk with Mr. Beastly over and over, around and around, each time remembering something he hadn't the previous time: the dog he tripped over, the Rialto, the vampire bat cloud, *"Good reporters don't need gadgets and gizmos!"* Nickel wasn't so sure he was a good reporter, or that he wanted to be, but a first draft of his interview was due the next day, and he would do his best.

When his eyes let him know that 15th Street had passed, he pulled the cord and a bell rang signaling the driver that a passenger wanted off. Nickel started down the aisle before the bus even stopped, banging his backpack into seats and other passengers. When the bus did stop, its double doors opened, and Nickel bounded down the steps into the street. He streaked toward home, his eyes scanning for obstacles. His ears were closed so that he could listen to Mr. Beastly's voice: *A city can be like a beehive.* He didn't hear the car motors and horns and doors opening and slamming. *Pedestrians become pests.* He went right by two people on the sidewalk who were yelling at each other at the top of their lungs without hearing them. He didn't even hear the siren or see the flashing lights of a fire truck as it inched its way up the street through the standstill traffic. *The traffic started backing up, so they widened the road some more.*

When Nickel reached the Gardenview Apartments, he dug his key out of his backpack, let himself in, and raced up the stairs, past Mrs. Ray with her cane. He said hello to her without thinking, without hearing his own voice or her reply, "Where's the fire?" He unlocked the door to his apartment, slammed it shut behind him, and dashed into his room. He took paper and pencil from his desk, sat down, and began furiously scribbling down everything he could remember.

It frightened him that his hand went so much slower

than his memory. He feared that as he wrote one thing, several more were being forgotten, that if he lingered too long over any one thought, others would simply evaporate, turn to steam, escape out his ears. He wrote like this for an hour, hunched over his desk, all his senses shut off, writing blindly, not feeling the breeze turning colder through his window, not seeing the light growing warmer, not hearing the front door opening and closing and his mom's voice calling out. He was locked on his subject, focused, projecting his memory onto paper.

"Nickel!" his mom said beside him. She shook his shoulder.

His mind's eye blinked. He looked up at her. "Can't talk now," he grunted. He didn't want to think about his mom or anything she might say. He had to concentrate.

"I've been calling you and calling you!" his mom said.

He could not shut her out. She had opened the darkroom door. The light from outside was ruining his pictures.

"I was standing at your door yelling your name!"

"Please, Mom!" Nickel said, using as few words as possible so as not to crowd out any in his head.

"All you had to do was answer! You could've just said you were busy! You could've —"

"*Leave me alone!*" Nickel shouted.

This took his mom by surprise. Nickel wasn't prone to outbursts, especially at her. He was surprised as well.

"I'm sorry," he said, closing his eyes. "I really have to write this down before I forget it."

His mom took a step back. "Oh," she said. She bowed her head slightly. "I see. I understand completely. Really I do. I'm sorry I disturbed you."

She wasn't being sarcastic; she was sincere. She'd been where Nickel was many times before. She knew what it was like to try to get something down before it was lost forever.

"I'm going off to work," she said. "I'll leave your dinner in the oven." She backed out the door, smiling at her son, though he didn't see. He was already back at it. She shut the door as quietly as she could and tiptoed out of the apartment.

                        ☙   ☙   ☙

"Did you turn yours in yet?" Inez asked Nickel the next day during lunch hour. They were sitting on top of the monkey bars.

Nickel shook his head. "We have English in the afternoon."

"Did you find out the secret?"

"No," he said. "But I know for sure there is one now."

"Why?"

"Because Mr. Beastly said things that didn't make sense. When I asked him questions, he didn't give me straight answers. He said the Beastly Arms owned him."

"*Owned* him?" Inez said, slipping through a gap in the bars and swinging upside down by her knees. "What does *that* mean?"

"He said a lot of buildings downtown owned him," Nickel said, looking down at her through the bars. Her braids were all tied into dozens of little pigtails all over her head. They hung downward like fringe. "He said when you're responsible for something, it owns you."

Inez swung in silence, mulling this over. Then she swung up, grabbed a bar, and pulled herself back up.

"Mrs. Bislimi said that her husband — he's dead — used to have a car that he was always fussing with. He'd get mad as a hornet if anybody came near it. Used to yell at the neighbor kids if they ever even *looked* at it. She said after a while she couldn't stand him anymore, he was so mean, so she told him to sell it or she didn't know what she was going to do."

"Did he?" Nickel asked.

"Nope," Inez said, letting go of the bar and dropping back into a swing. "He wrecked it."

"Is that how he died?"

"No!" Inez said with a giggle. "He didn't die for a long time after that."

"Did you use the tape recorder?" Nickel asked.

"Yeah," Inez said. "Didn't you?"

"He said I didn't need it. He said I'd remember everything. I didn't even remember my questions."

"You didn't ask him your *questions*?" She pulled herself up again. "You're supposed to."

"I know," Nickel said. "But he said a lot anyway. It took me forever to get it all down."

"He sure didn't say a lot when I saw him."

"I told you, he was sick then. He's better now."

The bell rang. Nickel and Inez climbed down to the blacktop.

"I hope you don't get a lower grade," Inez taunted. "You were *supposed* to ask your questions."

Nickel's shoulders slumped. "I know," he said.

"You got an *A*?" Inez said the next day after school. She looked shocked. Her mouth hung open.

When Nickel smiled at her, she punched him in the shoulder.

"An *A*? I can't believe it!"

"What did you get?" Nickel asked.

Inez giggled and ran down the front steps of the school. "An *A*!" She turned a cartwheel on the sidewalk.

Nickel laughed and ran down the steps after her.

"We'll both be in the paper!" he said.

He tried to return her punch, but she dodged and gave him a quick rabbit punch to the shoulder. Then she ducked away and ran off backward down the sidewalk, sticking her tongue out and turning cartwheels to let him know just how untouchable she was. Without realizing it, she cartwheeled right into the street. The signal was flashing DON'T WALK.

"Don't walk!" Nickel yelled.

A horn blew and brakes screeched and then there was a loud BOOMP! A blue car had hit Inez. Her body flew up into the air like a rag doll, then came down again.

Nickel froze. He blinked. He rubbed his eyes. He looked again. He didn't believe he'd seen what he'd seen. He didn't want to have seen it. His heart began to pound hard in his chest. In his ears. His feet began to run. Everything was completely different than it was a moment ago — stranger, crazier, scarier. Everything was wrong.

Nickel looked up from the floor when he heard his name called. His mom was walking quickly down the hall toward him, her arms swinging at her sides, the lines of fluorescent lights on the ceiling throwing her face into shadows. As she neared him, he rose out of his chair and opened his arms, waiting to be held. She wrapped her arms around him, squeezing him tight, her nose puffing into his ear, her lips pressing against his cheek.

"Are you all right?" she breathed.

It hadn't been Nickel who had been hit by the car, but he couldn't have felt any worse. He thought he might throw up.

"Maud!" Ms. Willamina said, coming out of Inez's room, her face all wet and swollen.

Nickel's mom stood and the two women hugged. Tears flowed down Ms. Willamina's cheeks in streams. Her body shook. Nickel's mom spoke in a low voice, rubbing Ms. Willamina's back slowly with her hands. Ms. Willamina pulled a tissue out from somewhere and dabbed her face. Her hand was shaking.

"She's still unconscious," she said more loudly than she'd intended, then cried out, "my poor child!"

Nickel's mom kept patting her back, saying, "Shhh, shhh."

The door to Inez's room opened again and Mr. Willamina stepped out. Cecil was asleep in his arms. Mr. Willamina smiled at Nickel's mom, his lips quivering.

Nickel's mom held out her arm and he joined the embrace, little Cecil in the middle of it.

"It's nobody's fault," Mr. Willamina kept saying. "Nobody's fault."

Nickel wandered past them, his eyes fixed on his feet as they moved down the hall. They weren't going anywhere in particular. They were just moving. His eyes weren't seeing. They were turned inward. He was seeing Inez. She was riding the concrete lion, swinging by her knees on the monkey bars, pulling him along behind her by his shirtsleeve. She was rabbit-punching. She was cartwheeling into the crosswalk against the light. She was flying into the air, like a rag doll.

Suddenly, Nickel found himself on his knees on the floor. He could hear the echo of footsteps rushing toward him. His eyes burned and his face was wet.

The next day was Friday. Nickel was supposed to go straight home from school and finish packing. He and his mom had been packing all week, a little each evening, except for the nights his mom waited tables. By Thursday, everything not needed for daily living had been put into boxes. They were moving out on Saturday. The Willaminas had offered to help before the accident, but they wouldn't be able to now. Nickel's mom chose not to ask his dad, saying she'd rather do it all by herself than to listen to him gripe all day. Mr. Kirkaby wasn't coming for the simple reason that Nickel had never told his mom he had offered to. Nickel and his mom didn't have a lot of stuff and what they did have wasn't very heavy. Only the beds, the dressers, the desks, and the couch would require two people to carry. Nickel was sure he and his mom could manage it alone. Even so, when Mr. Kirkaby asked him at school on Friday if they had enough help, Nickel surprised himself by saying no. At lunch, Mr. Kirkaby called Nickel's mom's office and left a message that he would be there the next day, ready and able.

Nickel did not go straight home after school. He went to the hospital. Inez was propped up in bed on pillows. There was a bandage covering her dozens of pigtails. One side of her face had a wide scrape that had begun to scab over. Her eyes were open. Bruises surrounded them.

"Hello, Nickel," Ms. Willamina said softly. She was sitting on a chair by Inez's bed with Cecil in her lap. She looked like she hadn't slept a wink the night before. "What have you got there?"

Nickel didn't look at her. He looked into Inez's eyes. They seemed different than before.

"Some books," he said. "I checked some out from the library for Inez."

He held them up for Inez to see. Her eyes lowered from his face to the books, but Nickel couldn't tell if they were seeing them. He couldn't tell if they were seeing anything. Then her eyes looked back up at him.

"It's me — Nickel," he said.

Her eyes rolled. "I'm not blind!" she said crossly.

"Inez!" Ms. Willamina said sternly. "You need to be polite to Nickel. He's your friend. He came to see you because he cares about you."

Inez just pursed her lips and blinked quickly several times at him.

"I'm sorry, Nickel," Mrs. Willamina said. "She's been like this all day." She glanced at Inez and Inez turned away and stared at the wall. "I guess she's just mad about getting hurt. I see that a lot down at the clinic. Someone comes in hurt and we fix them up and then they start hissing and snapping at everyone — the staff, their families. They're just so mad and they don't know who to be mad at, so they just pick the person closest to them at the time."

Inez snorted loudly.

"We're moving tomorrow," Nickel said meekly. He didn't know why he said it. It just came out. If he'd thought about it, he wouldn't have. It was sure to make Inez madder. But, with the accident and everything, he thought maybe she'd forgotten.

Inez got madder. She turned to face him, folded her arms and glared.

"I guess we won't be able to help you after all," Ms. Willamina said to Nickel. "Maybe Robert can come for a while."

"That's okay," Nickel said. "My teacher's going to come and help."

"Mr. *Kirkaby?*" Inez said, aghast. "He's coming to your *house?*"

Nickel nodded.

"You must be out of your mind!" Inez said.

"I-*nez*!" Ms. Willamina said.

"That's okay," Nickel said, turning to leave. "I'd better get going anyway. I have to get home and finish packing."

Inez blew air through her closed lips. She sounded like a horse.

"You pay no attention to her, Nickel," Ms. Willamina said. "And you tell your mama Robert will be by tomorrow if he can. Tell her we're sure sorry we can't be more help. And, here — let me have those books. I bet she'll want them later on."

Nickel handed them to her. "Bye, Inez," he said without looking at her.

She made the horse sound again.

Nickel heard Ms. Willamina scolding Inez as he went out the door. He wiped his eyes with his sleeve and made his way down the hall.

15

FOR breakfast the next morning, Nickel and his mom ate cold cereal, then washed their bowls and spoons and packed them away in the boxes with the rest of the kitchen stuff. Then they walked up to the deli on 17th Street and Nickel's mom bought a six-pack of soda and a few sandwiches to go.

On the way back to the Gardenview, Nickel thought about how it would be the last time that walking there would be walking home. After that, home would be One Tall Grass Drive, apartment 2E. That made him happy, but then they passed Sixto's newsstand and he felt a twinge of sadness.

"Good morning, Nickel and Nickel's mother!" Mrs. Zindel said as they passed her produce stand.

"Morning," Nickel's mom said with a nod.

They crossed Ivy at 17th, which Nickel had done thousands of times before. A man stepped out of Kleindienst's Bakery, shoving an enormous cinnamon bun into his mouth. It was Mr. Youdle. He motioned for them to stop.

"You're moving out today, right?" he asked through his food.

Nickel's mom nodded.

"I want you should be careful going down the stairs with things," he said. "I don't want nicks. And if you want your cleaning deposit back, leave it spotless, like it was before you moved in!"

"It wasn't exactly spotless when we moved in, Mr. Youdle," Nickel's mom said. "Now, if you'll excuse us." She began to walk away. Nickel followed.

"I want it spotless!" Mr. Youdle yelled from behind them. "Or I'll keep that deposit! Believe me!"

"Nice man, that Mr. Youdle," Nickel's mom said.

Nickel looked back over his shoulder. Mr. Youdle was pushing the rest of the bun into his mouth. Nickel was glad he wouldn't have to see — or hear — him anymore. He was glad that Mr. Youdle wouldn't be upsetting his mom all the time, raising the rent and making a fuss over nothing. *Mr. Beastly would never act like that,* Nickel thought. *Never.*

They turned onto Ira Monk Street. Mr. Willamina was up ahead, standing in front of their building, his hands in his pockets, staring out at the traffic in a daze. As they grew nearer, Nickel could see that his face was stubbly and his eyes were puffy.

"Hello, Robert," Nickel's mom said, setting her hand on his shoulder. "How's Inez?"

"Hi, Maud. Hi, Nickel," Mr. Willamina said, trying to smile. "She's home now. The doctor said she seems okay, just shaken up, but that we should watch her close. He says you never can tell with a head injury. We keep checking her eyes. They're not supposed to fix, you know. If they fix, we have to bring her back in. Her mama's with her. She seems okay. We just have to wait and see."

He was so serious that Nickel barely recognized him.

"You look so tired," Nickel's mom said to him. "We've got plenty of help. Nickel's teacher is coming, and some friends of mine from the college. They have a truck. Why don't you go on home and get some rest. We can manage."

But Mr. Willamina wouldn't hear of it. He wanted to help; he had come to help — that was what he kept saying. Finally Nickel's mom gave in and then offered him a sandwich or a soda but he said no, that he was fine, thanks.

Soon, Alma, Nickel's mom's friend from work, and her husband, Bob, drove up in a truck, and then Mr. Kirkaby came walking up Ira Monk Street, as if he was just a normal person. Nickel's mom introduced him to everyone and offered everyone a soda or a sandwich. Everyone said no thanks and they got to work carrying everything out of the apartment and into the truck. Nickel brought Miriam and her box out last.

During the week, Bob used his truck to deliver bread and rolls to stores and restaurants around town. It was big and boxy with only two seats, both in the cab. Bob and Alma sat in them. Nickel and his mom sat behind them on the floor. Miriam sat in Nickel's pocket. Mr. Kirkaby and Mr. Willamina sat on the couch in the back. Mr. Kirkaby asked Nickel not to mention this to Ms. Stonecipher, and Nickel agreed. It seemed strange having his teacher asking not to be told on, but no more strange than having him sitting on Nickel's couch in a bread truck in the middle of everything Nickel owned and driving down Ira Monk Street on a sunny Saturday morning.

"Turn left into that alley," Nickel's mom said after they'd traveled sixteen blocks. "Just past the light. Go slow. It's easy to miss."

Bob stopped the truck in front of the check-cashing place, put it into reverse, and backed into Tall Grass Drive. Nickel wished he could see the sky blue door and the brass nameplate, but the truck had no rear window. The truck inched backward until at last it stopped. Bob and Alma climbed out of the front. Nickel and his mom climbed out after them.

"Well, good morning!" Nickel heard a voice say cheerfully. It was Mr. Beastly's voice. Nickel decided he'd be wearing his suit and tie, maybe his hat. He sounded too cheerful to be wearing his robe.

"Welcome!" he was saying as Nickel came around the end of the truck. "Pleased to meet you!" Nickel was right: suit and tie, and he had his hat and watch on, too. Nickel's mom was introducing him to everyone and he was shaking their hands. He gave Nickel a wink.

"All right if we get started?" his mom asked.

Mr. Beastly smiled and withdrew a ring of keys from his pocket. "Here you are. A key to 2E and a key to the building. Two sets." He bowed as he handed them to Nickel's mom. "Let me know if you need anything."

The adults began pulling stuff out of the back of the truck and carrying it into the building.

"And where's your little friend?" Mr. Beastly asked, taking Nickel aside.

At first Nickel thought that he meant Inez again, and the thought made him sad. But then he realized he meant Miriam.

"She's here," Nickel said, patting his shirt pocket. "She didn't like the truck much."

"Understandably," Mr. Beastly said with a grin. "Would you like me to take care of her while you work?"

Nickel had never let anyone rat-sit Miriam before, but he dug her out of his pocket and handed her over to Mr.

Beastly without hesitating. Mr. Beastly held out his hand, in the center of which was, of course, a seed.

"I'll take good care of her," he said.

Nickel carried one of the boxes upstairs. He passed Mr. Kirkaby and Alma in the hall.

"Strange smell," Mr. Kirkaby was saying.

The door to 2E was open. Nickel carried the box inside just as his mom was coming out of the kitchen.

"That smell's still here," she said, wrinkling her nose. "I hope it isn't a permanent resident."

Nickel could smell it, too. It reminded him of Miriam's box.

"What's that stink?" Bob said as he set his load down in the living room. Bob was a tall man with black hair parted down the middle and a bulging belly. He had wide, black sideburns that he called muttonchops. Nickel thought he looked like a badger. Especially when he sniffed at the air.

An hour later, everything was out of the truck and in the apartment. Nickel's mom had Bob and Mr. Kirkaby set up Nickel's twin bed in the living room. Her plan was to make it a daybed. She had them put her queen-size bed in Nickel's room. She had a king-size four-poster in her room to sleep on. Then she offered the sandwiches and sodas again and this time everyone said yes. They all sat around the kitchen table, eating and drinking and talking.

Nickel went downstairs to collect Miriam. Mr. Beastly was sitting at the table in the lobby playing with her. The plants had perked up.

"Your mother has nice friends," Mr. Beastly said as he handed Miriam back.

Nickel nodded. "Mr. Willamina is Inez's dad. Remember Inez?"

"How could I forget?" Mr. Beastly said with a smile. "How is she?"

"Not so good," Nickel said, looking down. "She got hit by a car yesterday."

"Oh, how awful!" Mr. Beastly said. "Was she hurt badly?"

"The doctor says she's okay," Nickel said. "She's home from the hospital. Her parents are both nurses, so they take care of her. She has a bandage on her head and some cuts and bruises. The doctor says you never can tell with a head injury."

Mr. Beastly shook his head. "I often wonder why automobiles are allowed in the city at all," he said. "It's like letting a herd of elephants into your kitchen."

Nickel imagined the streets without cars. He imagined no traffic lights, no parking meters, no honking horns. No smutch. But then he wondered how they would have gotten their stuff across town without Bob's truck. He imagined Mr. Kirkaby and Mr. Willamina carrying the couch sixteen blocks down Ira Monk Street.

"Well, I hope she's better soon," Mr. Beastly said. "Send her my best wishes for a speedy recovery."

Nickel nodded. "I just can't believe it happened to her," he said. "She's so careful. She always does things right. I'm the one that never looks where I'm going. It was supposed to be me, I think." He looked down at the floor. "I wish it had been."

Mr. Beastly set his hand on Nickel's shoulder. "That's not the way it works, my boy," he said. "Accidents can happen to anyone, no matter how careful you are. No one is perfect, you know. Everyone has lapses in attention from time to time. The problem is, with all these two-ton automobiles around, even a momentary distraction can result in tragedy." He looked Nickel in the eye. "Still, it probably wouldn't hurt to look where you're going. That's why your eyes are in front." He grinned and Nickel smiled.

"Is everything okay up there?" Mr. Beastly asked, gesturing toward the ceiling.

"Uh-huh," Nickel said. "They all say it smells, though."

"Smells? Smells like what?"

"I think it smells like Miriam's box."

Mr. Beastly nodded and stared up at the ceiling. He looked as if he were troubled about something, then he looked back down at Nickel and said, "The previous tenants had pets. Guinea pigs, I think. I'm sure the smell will go away soon enough."

Nickel thought about how he and his mom had looked at the apartment a month before and how it had been empty then — no tenants, no guinea pigs — and how it had smelled just the same. Then, Mr. Beastly had said it was his jacket.

"Tell your mom a few plants might help," Mr. Beastly said. "Some flowers, too, maybe."

"Okay," Nickel said. "I'm going back up now."

"Yes, yes," Mr. Beastly said, his troubled look disappearing. "Go! Show Miriam her new home!"

Everyone was just heading out when Nickel stepped through the door. Bob and Alma left first, then Mr. Willamina. Mr. Kirkaby offered to stay and help unpack.

"That's not necessary, Duncan," Nickel's mom said, smiling.

"*Duncan,*" Nickel grumbled under his breath.

"It's no trouble," Mr. Kirkaby said. "I live only a few blocks from here. I have a great big stack of math homework waiting for me to correct, so I'm in no rush to get there. I won't put anything away. I'll just unwrap. I'm very good at unfolding paper. It comes from intercepting notes in class."

Nickel's mom laughed.

While Mr. Kirkaby unwrapped kitchen things and Nickel's mom put them away, Nickel got to work on his new room. He put his books back on his bookshelves, arranging them by kingdom, phylum, class, order, and species, according to the rules of animal taxonomy. Nearly all his books were about animals. A few were about photography.

"Knock, knock," Mr. Kirkaby said, poking his head in Nickel's doorway. "May I come in?"

Nickel looked up from his books, stunned. *His teacher was in his room!* The only response he could manage was something between a shrug, a nod, and a grunt.

"What are these?" Mr. Kirkaby said, sifting through Nickel's cloud drawings on his dresser.

"Just drawings," Nickel said.

"Are they clouds?" Mr. Kirkaby asked, holding one up.

"That's a lobster," Nickel said.

Mr. Kirkaby held the drawing closer, then held it at arm's length. "Oh, I see it!" he said with a laugh. He picked up another one. "What's this one?"

"A termite."

Mr. Kirkaby nodded. "It's like the constellations," he said. "People looked up at the stars and saw all these animals — bears and oxen and dogs — just by connecting the dots." He set the drawings down. "I just came in to say good-bye. I'm heading home."

"Good-bye," Nickel said.

"Your Mr. Beastly is an interesting man," Mr. Kirkaby said. "Your interview did him justice. Did you ever find out his secret?"

Nickel shook his head. "Not yet."

"Well, remember, sometimes people keep things to themselves for good reasons. Sometimes they don't want anyone to try to find them out."

Nickel stared up at him, hoping that he was absolutely and completely wrong.

16

NICKEL lay awake that night in his new queen-size bed, unable to fall asleep. There were too many things on his mind — too many pictures. The darkness and stillness of his room provided no distractions. Unlike the Gardenview, there were no noises from the street, no streetlights. All he could hear in his new room was the occasional muffled siren going by. Everything else came from inside, from memory. He heard Inez's voice, his mom's, his dad's, Mr. Kirkaby's, Mr. Beastly's. None of them helped him sleep. On the contrary, they made him restless. Too much was unsettled, too much, mysterious. Would Inez be all right? Was she really only angry at him because she was hurt, or was she mad at him for moving away? What would his dad say when he saw the Beastly Arms? Could he ruin things, make them move? Would his mom marry his teacher? Would Nickel *ever* discover Mr. Beastly's secret? *Was* there a secret? All of these questions were accompanied by a stream of images and the blackness of his high ceiling was the perfect screen for the projection of these persistent visions.

Maybe he was out of his mind, as Inez said. He and his mom now lived in the Beastly Arms and it was all because of him. The day before he dragged Inez downtown with him he had wanted nothing more than to stay right where he was, in his old neighborhood. He had been hoping his mom would change her mind and decide to stay in the Gardenview. And then, suddenly, just because he and his mom had accidentally gone up a dead-end alley, he had done all he could to get her to move, and not only out of the neighborhood, but downtown. And to where? To the Beastly Arms, a place — a *strange* place — run by a person — a *strange* person — about whom he knew practically nothing. And he'd succeeded. They had moved. All their stuff was in the Beastly Arms. They now lived downtown, where Inez wasn't even allowed to go.

Why had his mom listened to him? Why had she followed? She knew that he never knew where he was going. Nickel saw himself on the ceiling, circling downtown, trying to find the Beastly Arms. He saw himself tripping over the dog on his walk with Mr. Beastly. He saw Inez in the domed hall of the library. *Earth to Nickel!* she was saying. *Come in, Nickel!* A person had to be a fool to follow him. Most of the time he didn't even see what was right in front of him.

How can I find the secret? he thought. *I could trip right over it without even noticing!*

Sometimes people keep things to themselves for good reasons, Nickel heard Mr. Kirkaby say. *Sometimes they don't want anyone to try to find them out.*

What had made Nickel think that Mr. Beastly wanted him to find it? What had made Nickel go back to the Beastly Arms at all?

Nickel sat up in bed.

"Miriam," he murmured.

She was beside him on the bed, curled up on the sweatshirt he'd worn that day. His eyes had adjusted enough to the darkness to see her dim, soft outline. She was gnawing on a seed. He leaned over and pressed his nose in close to her. She tickled it with her whiskers. At least now he could keep her without fear of being evicted.

What your Mr. Youdle doesn't understand is that, whether he's aware of it or not, all of his tenants are animals! Mr. Beastly said again in Nickel's mind.

"It's no use," Nickel said out loud. "I can't sleep."

He eased out of bed and slipped on his robe, then, tucking Miriam into a pocket, he moved slowly across his room, his hands outstretched, feeling around like antennae. He managed to reach the door without stubbing his toes or tripping over anything, then fumbled for the knob, turned it, and stepped out into the hall.

The hallway was pitch black — blacker than his room. Nickel reached a hand out to his side, touching the wall with his fingertips, and tiptoed down the hall. He could only hope that there wasn't anything on the floor. There were no lights on up ahead. He figured his mom was asleep in her room behind him. Her bedroom light was out. Then, to his right, his fingers ran over the frame of the front door, then onto the doorknob.

Nickel hadn't known where he was heading when he'd decided to leave his room, but he certainly hadn't intended on leaving the apartment. It had seemed more likely to him he would end up in the kitchen for a mid-night snack. But there he was, turning the knob on the front door. When he tried to pull it open, though, it wouldn't budge. It was locked. He felt around for a latch of some kind and found the small, oval knob of the dead bolt. When he turned it there was a *clunk!* — which made him wince. He stood still in the dark, waiting for sounds from his mom's bedroom, but when none came, he slowly pulled the door open and stepped outside. He left the door ajar behind him.

Still unsure of where he was going — or why — Nickel elected somehow to go right, toward the stairs. This hallway was even darker than the one in the apart-ment. It was like a darkroom. Nickel couldn't see a thing. The floor creaked as he moved slowly along, careful to stay in the center, not wishing to collide with the potted plants on pedestals along the walls. Miriam began to stir in his robe pocket. She started chattering nervously. Nickel froze. From his left, he heard something squeak-ing. It sounded a bit like a rusty wheel on a shopping cart. It was soon joined by another: two squeaking, rusty shopping-cart wheels. Then three. Then four. *It must be the whole cart,* Nickel thought.

Then all at once the squeaking stopped. Miriam fell silent and still. Nickel did the same for a moment, then continued on down the hall, his heart beating in his throat.

Another sound arose a few steps later — a ruffling, like someone shaking out a bed sheet. Someone somewhere said, "Who?" Nickel worried that maybe one of the tenants had heard him tiptoeing down the hall and, thinking that he was a burglar, was calling the police. He scooted down the hall as quickly — but as quietly — as he could, wondering as he went why he was going *down* the hall instead of back *up* the hall to his apartment. He didn't know what it was that was telling him what to do. It felt like his stomach.

Your gut is nature talking, Mr. Beastly said in Nickel's head. *Listen to it.*

Soon, up ahead and to his right, Nickel could make out a rectangle that was slightly lighter than its surroundings. He assumed it was a doorway. He hoped it was the stairwell, and not one of the apartment doors, opened, a tenant ready to pounce on him. As he got closer he saw the outlines of the stairs going down. It was lighter downstairs.

The skylight in the lobby, he thought.

To the left of the stairs going down were stairs going up. Nickel had never gone higher than the second floor. He wondered how many floors there were. He groped for the banister, found it, then, using the handrail, pulled himself up the stairs to a landing. He turned right and climbed the next set of stairs up to the third floor. It was as dark as the second. To his right were more stairs, going up. He climbed them to the fourth floor, then climbed more to the fifth, then the sixth. On the seventh, the smell — the one that had reminded him of Miriam's box — was stronger. He wondered if it had been getting stronger all along without his noticing it. It was even stronger on the eighth floor. On the ninth, when he turned right, there was a door. It was closed. But it wasn't locked. Inside it were more stairs. They weren't carpeted like the others. They were wooden. At the top of them, instead of hitting a landing, Nickel hit another door — with his head. He opened the door, stepped through, and found himself on the roof. Above was a dark twinkling sky.

People looked up at the stars and saw all these animals, Mr. Kirkaby had said.

The stars were faint due to the glow of the city's lights, but Nickel could make out some of the brighter ones.

"That's a pelican," he said softly, connecting the stars with his finger. "And that's a praying mantis."

He sat down on the cold cement roof, wrapping the ends of his robe around his bare feet. Miriam climbed out of his pocket and began searching for food. Mostly what she found was dirt and soot and bird droppings, but she did manage to find a few seeds left behind by pigeons.

Nickel noticed that many of the animals in the stars overlapped: the tapir over the swordfish, the assassin bug over the pelican. Then, as he was connecting the final dots on a koala in a straw hat, his vision was briefly obscured by a flash — a bright white flash. It had come from below.

Nickel lowered his hand and scanned the sky for what had caused it. He had only seen the flash briefly, but he was pretty sure it had been some kind of bird.

I'd say it was a bat, he thought to himself, *but I don't know of any white bats. There are nocturnal birds, of course, like goatsuckers and whip-poor-wills. But it was so big.*

Nickel suddenly became aware of a strong vibration against his hip, and when he looked down he found Miriam curled up tightly in his robe pocket, shaking like a leaf. He hadn't even seen her climb back in.

"What is it?" he whispered to her. He'd never seen her so frightened, not on the subway, not even when there was a cat around.

And then the white flash flashed again. It dove from above, white and silent, like a ghost, then leveled off and flew directly over Nickel's head.

"A barn owl!" Nickel gasped.

The owl circled overhead, its enormous eyes gazing down, its talons tucked under. Nickel instinctively placed his hand over Miriam in his pocket. She trembled violently against his palm. The owl turned a few more circles then tilted its wide, outstretched wings and swooped away from the building, out over the city, and was gone.

I should have known! Nickel said to himself. *Big, white, and flies at night! An OWL!*

He replayed in his mind's eye what he'd seen. It was difficult to believe. Yet the details were all there: the snowy feathers, the curling talons, the strong beak. He hadn't imagined it. He had seen it. What's more, he wasn't the only one; Miriam had seen it, too.

He opened the pocket of his robe to see how she was holding up. Her head twitched quickly first one way then another. Her eyes were as big as thumbtacks. Nickel reached in and stroked the top of her tiny head with his fingertip.

"It's gone," he said.

Miriam leaned into his hand.

Nickel rubbed his bare feet together and realized they were practically numb from the cold. "We better get inside," he said to Miriam.

As they were crossing back across the roof to the stairs, a sound arose from below somewhere. It was a very particular sound that Nickel knew well. It was the sound of a wood-framed window sliding open: shhhhh-THUNK! He walked to the edge of the building, which had a two-foot-high ledge along it. Nickel knelt down and leaned over on it. He saw that the Beastly Arms was bordered on three sides by buildings, all of them shorter than itself, and only one of them — the one to his right — actually touching it. The building on the left was separated from the Beastly Arms by a small gap, the space he had seen from his window, the one with the weeds and bushes at the bottom. With more light, Nickel was sure he would see that the building was made of red brick. The building directly ahead of him was made of a silvery metal. It glistened in the starlight. It was separated from the Beastly Arms by a much wider space than the building on the left. Nickel strained to see what lay far below in the gap, but it was too dark.

Then he heard another window sliding open. When he

looked down, a swarm of dark creatures came rushing up out of the dark — *directly at him!* He reeled back away from the ledge and, a second later, they surged up over it, flapping and chirping, then scattering out over his head. A smile spread across his face as he watched them disappear into the night sky.

"Bats!"

He peeked cautiously back over the ledge. The wall below him was filled with windows. He counted six in each horizontal row. He couldn't count the number of rows because they faded off into the darkness below. Each row of windows had a white stone ledge that ran the length of the building. Creeping up the wall and around all the windows were vines. Nickel thought he heard leaves rustling, and a cheeping sound.

Miriam responded with a cheep of her own. She clawed at Nickel's robe, trying to poke through it to his flesh. Nickel leaned back from the ledge and peeked in at her.

"You want to go inside?" he asked.

Her eyes stared up at him, big and black and imploring.

He carried her back into the building, warming her

with his hand as he went. He had to keep count of the floors in his head as he made his way down. They all looked the same: black. When he hit the second floor, he tiptoed down the middle of the hall to 2E. Then, at last, back in his room, he set Miriam in her box. She dove into her seed cup. Trembling had given her an appetite.

Nickel lay down on his bed on his back, staring at the black ceiling above him, his heart beating so fast that he thought he'd never fall asleep again.

But he did.

17

THE last thing Nickel wanted to do the next day was to spend it with his dad. He didn't want to set foot outside of the Beastly Arms. He had mysteries to solve. But it was that Sunday of the month and there was no way out of it. His mom wouldn't say that he had to stay home and unpack, or that he had to go with her to the Gardenview and clean. She wouldn't even say he was sick. His mom never said he was sick when he wasn't.

"You've *got* to be kidding me!" his dad said when his mom opened the door for him. "This is the worst neighborhood in town! Are you crazy? Don't you know what's going on out there!"

"No, what?" Nickel's mom said, her arms crossed.

"What? *What?* Are you *kidding* me?" He glanced down at Nickel, who was standing behind her, ready to be taken away. "There are guys out there, smoking . . . *you know* . . . in doorways. There are needles on the sidewalks, for crying out loud! And there are . . . you know . . . *women* . . . on the corners! And *people,* lying right on the *ground!*"

Nickel could see that it made his dad uncomfortable to be discussing these things in front of him, but what his dad didn't realize was that none of what he was talking about was anything Nickel wasn't aware of. He had lived in the city all his life. The prostitutes and the drug users and the homeless people were part of the habitat.

"Well, like it or not, Nick, this is where we live!" Nickel's mom said, her posture stiffening. "You think this is where I *want* us to be? I work as hard as I can, day and night some days, and this is the best I can do. Maybe Nickel would be safer living with you out in Oak Hollow, but he *doesn't* live with you! He lives with *me!* And besides —"

That was as much as Nickel heard of the conversation. He tuned them out. He knew the rest by heart anyway. He wandered away into the living room, to the couch, where he sat looking up at the Henri Cartier-Bresson photograph in its new hanging place. It calmed him to see all the children there, through the hole in the wall. He wondered whether where they lived was safe. That boy on the crutches, walking through the rubble — was he safe? And those boys wrestling — were they? Were there needles in the rubble? Were there drug dealers? Gunshots? Blue cars? His dad would say it was a bad neighborhood. The walls were crumbling and the children were playing in the street. So why were they laughing?

Nickel stared longest, as usual, at the boy with the dark eye sockets, the one who seemed to be looking at the camera. *Maybe he's not seeing anything,* Nickel thought. *Maybe he's looking in — remembering. Maybe he's not really there at all.*

When the arguing eventually stopped, Nickel's parents stood facing each other, breathing hard, their cheeks reddened, each knowing they had more to say, but that there was no use in saying it. Everything had been said far too many times before. Nickel got up from the couch.

"Ready?" he said.

Nickel spent the afternoon at his dad's house in Oak Hollow. There was an important open on TV. Nickel sat on the couch with his dad pretending to watch the men hitting the tiny white balls around in the bright green grass, but all he could think of were bats and owls.

"We should play some golf again soon," Nickel's dad said during a commercial break. "It'd do you good to get out into nature."

Golf has nothing whatsoever to do with nature! Nickel remembered Mr. Beastly saying. *Nature likes a mess.*

"Okay," Nickel said.

And then something in one of the commercials caught his attention. A photographer was taking a quick succession of pictures of a baseball player swinging a bat. It was a night game, and so, with every exposure, there was a flash. The photographer was using an electronic strobe.

It gave Nickel an idea.

He barged right up to his mom when he got home. She was in the kitchen, leaning against the sink, her back toward him.

"Can I borrow a long lens and a strobe?" he asked.

His mom turned around and Nickel saw that she had the phone pressed up to her ear. She held a forefinger up.

"Just a minute, Duncan," she said into the phone. "Nickel's home." She placed her palm over the mouthpiece. "What is it?" she asked Nickel.

"Is that Mr. *Kirkaby*?" Nickel asked, his eyes wide. "Am I in trouble?"

His mom shook her head. "We're just talking. What do you need?"

Nickel couldn't remember.

"I'll be off in a sec," his mom said. She uncovered the mouthpiece and resumed her conversation with Nickel's teacher.

" 'Just a minute, *Duncan*,' " Nickel muttered to himself as he left the kitchen. He plodded off to his room and got his camera from out of his dresser drawer. "Film!" he said suddenly. "I need film!"

He ran back to the kitchen. His mom was just hanging up the phone.

"So, what did you need?" she asked.

"Can I use your eighty-five millimeter lens and your strobe?" he asked.

His mom laughed. "You haven't taken a picture in a month! Gwendolyn keeps asking me where you are."

"I know," Nickel said. "Can I?"

"Sure," his mom said. She set her arm around his shoulders and led him into the living room. "Do you need them right this second?"

He wouldn't really need them until later that night — much later, after she was asleep — but he didn't want to tell her that.

"No, I guess not," he said with a sigh.

"A long lens," his mom said, sitting down on the couch and guiding Nickel down beside her. "Close-ups of individual raindrops, maybe? What's the flash for?"

"I don't want to say right now," Nickel said. To his mom, that was usually an acceptable answer.

"Okay," she said. She gave him a kiss on the head. "Duncan just called to see how everything was going, if we needed anything. He's very nice."

Nickel nodded. He didn't want to think about it.

"I have homework," he said, standing up.

"That's not what Duncan said."

Nickel knew nothing good could come of this parent–teacher relationship.

"Well, it's not really *homework*," he said. "It's more like *studying*."

His mom smiled. "Okay. I'll get the lens and the strobe out for you in the morning."

"No!" Nickel said louder than he should have. It made his mom start.

"You need them sooner?" she said, beginning to laugh.

"Tonight," Nickel said, trying to act as if it wasn't as big a deal as he'd made it sound. He didn't want to arouse her suspicion. "If that's okay, I mean. I want to do some tests."

"All right," his mom said, smiling. "I'll get them out after dinner."

      ॐ   ॐ   ॐ

The journey back through the pitch-black apartment building that night went much more smoothly. The doorknobs were easier to find; so was the dead bolt. As in the darkroom, with practice he could find things without light.

The hall was just as noisy as before. Again, the floor creaked, the squeaks squeaked, someone said, "Who?" Again, the smells were stronger the higher he went. On the seventh floor it was so strong that his eyes watered. On the eighth, his nose and throat began to burn. He covered his mouth and nose with his arm and mounted the remaining stairs two at a time. It wasn't until he was on the roof that he could lower it.

There were clouds in the sky this time. The stars gleamed through them like streetlights through fog. The night air was cold again, but Nickel's feet weren't. This time he'd worn socks and slippers. He sat down on the cement, took the strobe out of his robe pocket and attached it to the camera. He flicked it on and it made a soft, high-pitched squealing sound. Miriam poked her head out of his other pocket to see who it was.

"It's just the flash," Nickel whispered to her.

When its "ready" light came on, Nickel pressed the test button. The roof lit up. Miriam squealed and ducked back down into his pocket.

Nickel checked the strobe's exposure meter. It said he should shoot at f5.6. At that f-stop — and focusing at forty feet — everything between seventeen and fifty feet away would be sharp. Nickel had no way of knowing how far away the owl would be when — or if — it flew by again. His plan was to let the bird get more than twenty feet away and then shoot. That way it would be in focus for sure. The long lens would magnify the image so that it wouldn't appear far away in the photograph; it would look as if the owl had been right in Nickel's face. He set the aperture to f5.6 and the shutter speed to one-twenty-fifth of a second, standard for shooting with the flash, then he brought the camera up to his eye, set his elbows on his knees, his finger on the trigger, and waited for the barn owl to return.

He waited a long time. A very long time. He waited so

long that he began to wonder why he'd ever thought that the owl would reappear at all.

Are barn owls even creatures of habit? he wondered. He knew that they preferred one roost and that they defended their territory vigilantly. But he had no reason to believe the owl's roost was nearby, or that it had a routine to its patrol. No reason at all.

He did have a hunch, though. And a hope.

Then, at last, after Nickel had been waiting for over an hour, the white flash returned. He saw it in his viewfinder and instantly backed away from the camera to see. The owl rose up over the edge of the roof as it had the night before and sailed up into the sky, like a ghost. Nickel grinned ear to ear.

Miriam, who had ventured out in search of food, scrambled back across the roof and dove into Nickel's pocket.

As the owl began to circle, Nickel brought the camera back up to his eye and followed the bird's path through his viewfinder. He aimed ahead of it a bit, leading it, and then waited for the owl to appear. At the first glimpse of white he pressed the trigger. The shutter clicked; the flash flashed. Instinctively, Nickel twisted the film advance.

It twisted too easily.

"Oh, no!" Nickel gasped. "Didn't I put film in?"

He looked down at Miriam in his pocket. She didn't answer.

At first, Nickel couldn't understand how this could have happened. He remembered going to the kitchen for film. He remembered it vividly. But he couldn't exactly remember opening the refrigerator. He couldn't exactly remember taking any film out. He definitely couldn't remember loading the camera.

Then he understood. It wasn't so hard to believe. Between the time he'd made up his mind to go to the kitchen for the film and the time he'd returned, he'd completely forgotten about it. It wasn't the first time he'd done something like that.

Earth to Nickel! he heard Inez saying in his head. *Come in, Nickel!*

The owl finished circling and then, with a mighty flap

of its wings, soared out over the neighboring buildings and vanished into the clouds.

"It's okay," he said to Miriam, patting her through his robe. "It's gone." He sighed.

He flicked off the strobe, set the camera down on the cement, and sat there a moment, wishing so much that he could remember simple little things once in a while (like putting film in his camera and looking where he was going) when suddenly he was struck by a thought.

I'll get it when it comes back!

He jumped to his feet and ran across the roof toward the stairs. As he reached the door, a swarm of bats surged up over the ledge to his right, squealing and flapping and scattering off into the sky.

Nickel's shoulders slumped. "Great," he said. "Just great."

He made his way down the stairs as quickly as he could, holding his arm up over his nose and mouth (the smell was still there). He wished he were a bat and could fly down to his apartment, through the kitchen window, and to the fridge for film, but he realized that if he were a bat, he wouldn't be able to open the refrigerator door. Not to mention load the camera.

As he passed the fifth-floor landing and started down the steps to the fourth, he grew impatient and started to run — and promptly stumbled. He only fell down a few steps before he was able to stop himself, but it was enough to prevent him from trying that again. At the second floor, he did allow himself to walk-run down the hall, but when he grazed one of the potted plants with his sleeve, he slowed down. Then, as he neared the door to 2E, he stopped short. There was a halo of bright glowing around the door. His mom was up.

Nickel peeked inside and saw that the light was coming from his mom's room at the end of the hall. Her door was shut. He figured she probably couldn't sleep and was up reading. She often did that. Sometimes she went to the kitchen for tea. Since the front door had still been ajar, as he'd left it, she probably hadn't done that tonight. Not yet anyway.

Nickel stood in the hall a minute trying to decide what

to do. He could just tiptoe back to his room and go to bed, or he could tiptoe into the kitchen, get a roll of film, and return to the roof. The camera was still up there. Maybe the owl would return. Or the bats. But if he went back up, there was a chance his mom might decide to go to the kitchen for tea after all, and then she'd surely see that the door was open. Maybe she'd figure that one of them had absentmindedly left it open. She'd probably figure it had been him. Regardless, she would definitely shut, and lock, the door. Then again, she *might* think something was wrong — that there was a burglar, maybe, or a kidnapper — and check in on Nickel to see that he was all right. Then he'd be in for it for sure.

Nickel ran all of this through his mind a few times, then tiptoed inside to the kitchen and took a roll of film from the fridge. Miriam squealed in his pocket as the cold shot through her bones. (She was not having a particularly enjoyable night.) Nickel tucked the film in his pocket, tiptoed back to his room, got his keys out of his backpack, then tiptoed back to the front door. He stepped out into the hallway, pulled the door shut quietly behind him, and then locked it with his key. The sound of the dead bolt clunking made him wince.

I must be crazy, he thought as he made his way back down the dark, creaky hall toward the stairs.

No one said, "Who?" this time.

He loaded his camera faster than he ever had in his whole life, then he flicked the strobe back on. It squealed low and whiny. Miriam remained in her pocket. She'd learned. Nickel checked the camera's settings. He propped his elbows on his knees and leaned his eye up to the viewfinder.

"Come back, owl," he said. "Now I'm ready."

But the owl didn't come back. Nickel waited for two hours. Even in his slippers, his feet began to freeze. He felt tired and achy from sitting in such an awkward position for such a long time on such a hard, cold roof. But he couldn't go in. Not now. Not after all he'd gone through.

An hour later, he fell asleep, still sitting up, his closed eye pressed up against the viewfinder. Then, after another hour, he was jolted awake by what he thought was Miriam, squealing in his ear. When he looked around for her, he discovered she was still hunkered down in his pocket, shaking like a leaf. He covered her with his hand. The squealing didn't stop.

He looked down at the strobe and saw that the red "ready" light was still on. He brought it up to his ear. It wasn't squealing. It only did that when it was warming up. The sound was coming from somewhere else.

He tried to stand, but his legs wouldn't straighten out. His knees were frozen. He massaged them until he was able to unbend them, then got up on his feet. They were frozen, too. He hobbled across the roof to the ledge. The squealing grew louder. He knelt down and peered over the ledge at the rows of windows below.

And he saw something — a small, dark something — move. Then he saw another one. Then another. Whatever the things were, they appeared to be shimmying down the vines. Nickel wished he could see them better. He wished he had a flashlight.

A flash!

He propped his elbows on the ledge and brought the camera up to his eye. He hoped everything was still set correctly. He had no time to check. The strobe's "ready" light was glowing. And there was film in the camera. Nickel aimed the camera down at the wall and shot.

For one-twenty-fifth of a second, the narrow space between the buildings lit up as if lightning had struck, then was dark as before. A chorus of screeching and chattering rose up out of the chasm. The stench Nickel had smelled earlier in the building suddenly filled his nostrils. His eyes burned. His nose and throat burned. He stepped back away from the ledge, wiping his eyes with his sleeve. The smell pursued him. He rushed for the door, and stumbled down the stairs, his arm over his nose and mouth. Finally, on the fourth floor, the stench began to weaken. By the time he reached his front door, it had become only a faint aroma. He twisted the doorknob and pushed the door.

It wouldn't budge.

She must have gotten up! he thought, panicked. *She must have shut the door and locked it!*

He didn't know what to do. He paced back and forth

in the hall. Should he knock? Which would be worse: having to spend the night in the hall or having to explain to his mom why he was out there in the first place? He decided it would be better not to knock, to sleep in the hall and come up with some reason why he had gone out tomorrow, after he'd had some sleep. Maybe he could say he'd gone out in the morning. She wouldn't be angry if he went out during the day. Still, he had no idea how he was going to explain the door being locked. It only locked with the key, and if he'd had the key to lock it then he could have just as easily —

"Earth to Nickel!" he said, slapping himself on the forehead. He dug into his pocket and pulled out his keys. "Come in, Nickel!"

18

WHEN the lunch bell rang the next day, all the other kids in class rushed out into the crowded hall, but Nickel stayed seated at his desk. He stared ahead at the chalkboard without seeing it. What he saw was the night sky over the Beastly Arms. He saw the owl and the bats. He did not see Mr. Kirkaby standing over him, or hear him saying, "Mr. Dill? Mr. Dill?"

After lunch, on the playground, some of the kids came up to the monkey bars, wanting to hear about Inez and the blue car, wanting to hear about what Nickel had seen. But Nickel didn't hear them. He just stared ahead, rolling a small aluminum canister in his palms, seeing pictures of small, dark things shimmying up vines, and waiting for the final bell.

"Where have you been?" Gwendolyn asked later that afternoon in the equipment cage.

Nickel shrugged.

"Well, it's good to see you," she said with a smile. "What do you need?"

Nickel told her, then took the key and the equipment and let himself into Room C. He quickly arranged everything so he could find it in the dark, then shut out the light. Miriam stirred in his pocket.

"Good morning," Nickel said to her, stroking her tiny head with his finger.

He slid the magazine open, carefully transferred the film onto a reel, then set it into the tank and screwed on the lid. He only had the one roll to develop. In fact, he only had one exposure.

He switched the light back on and prepared the chemicals for developing. He poured the soup, then the stop bath, then the fix into the tank. Then he washed the film and hung it on the drying line. Except for one small rectangle, the film was black. Nickel turned his head sideways, trying to make out what was in the rectangle, the one picture, trying to see what the dark forms on the wall had been. But he couldn't. They were far too small to make out. Once the film was dry, he could look at it with a magnifier. That wouldn't be for an hour or so, though.

He shut the drying cabinet, locked up the darkroom, and went down the hall to his mom's office. She was sitting at her desk, talking with Alma. Alma's pointy nose twitched when she spoke. That, along with her deep, dark eyes and her short, gray hair gave her the appearance of an opossum.

"Well, hello!" his mom said. "What are you doing here?"

"Developing," Nickel said.

"Is that a fancy way of saying growing up?" Alma quipped.

Nickel's mom laughed. Nickel didn't. He just dismissed it as one of those things that adults sometimes say.

"We thought we'd go out for Thai food tonight," his moms said. "You and me and Alma and Bob. Okay?"

Nickel nodded.

His mom pinched her lips with her fingers. "And I thought I might invite Duncan, too," she said.

Nickel's mouth dropped open. "*Why?*"

"I thought he might like to join us."

Nickel groaned.

"I don't blame you, Nickel," Alma said with a grin. "When I was a kid, I wouldn't have wanted my mom dating my teacher, either."

"It's not a *date*," Nickel's mom said, grimacing at Alma. "It's *dinner*. With *friends*."

"I'm going to the library," Nickel said. He turned to leave.

"Nickel!" his mom called after him. "We're hungry! We'd like to get going!"

Nickel stopped. "I want to wait for my film to dry," he said without turning around.

"But that won't be for at least an hour," his mom said. "Why don't you pick it up tomorrow?"

Nickel pouted. He stomped his foot. "I want to wait for them," he whined. He never acted like this around anyone except his mom.

She stood and crossed the room to him. "I can see they're important to you," she said softly. "But can't they wait for one day?"

Nickel snorted then mumbled, "Oh, okay."

"Why don't you go to the library while I make my call?" his mom said. "I'll come get you in a few minutes."

Nickel walked away down the hall. "I have to turn in my equipment," he said over his shoulder.

He heard Alma laugh. He couldn't imagine what was funny.

The adults spoke noisily to each other during dinner, allowing Nickel to forget his cares and focus on his pad thai. It was one of his favorites. He loved the noodles and the crunchy bamboo shoots and the peanuts. He loved to arrange each bite just so. Sometimes he wanted it oniony, other times minty, others, nutty. The combinations were endless.

Mr. Kirkaby accepted Nickel's mom's invitation. He ordered pad thai as well, but ate it thoughtlessly, stuffing random forkfuls into his mouth between sentences. For the first time, Nickel didn't think of him only as his teacher. He didn't seem so big and important. He was just a man eating dinner, like any other man.

Nickel was last to finish eating. The server took his plate away and returned with a dish of fortune cookies. Everyone took one and cracked them open. Nickel's read:

You have many secrets. Protect them.

"What's yours say, Nickel?" Mr. Kirkaby asked him.

"It's a secret," Nickel said, folding it in half.

School the next day went much as it had the day before. Inez wasn't there. Nickel was, but wasn't. He sat alone on the monkey bars during morning recess, lunch hour, and afternoon recess.

Mr. Kirkaby cancelled his planned afternoon English lesson, instead leading the class outside to the thin row of trees behind the playground, where they all sat in the grass and listened to him read a story. He read *The Light Princess* by George MacDonald, which was about a princess that could not stay on the ground. Nickel, who had assumed that the "light" in the title referred to an absence of darkness, not weight, nevertheless enjoyed the story very much. Usually he had a hard time concentrating on a story read aloud to him. Something would always trigger some memory, some picture, some voice, and he would drift off into his own head. But this one held his attention until the end. This was all the more unusual considering all that he had on his mind. It was nice just lying on his back and letting things go for a while. He gazed up at the sky, watching the story play itself out against the clouds. The princess, as he envisioned her, bore a remarkable resemblance to Inez.

"Boy," Scott whispered to Nickel at the end of the story, "Mr. K. is sure in a good mood today!"

Nickel glanced over at Mr. Kirkaby and saw that his eyes were glistening.

After school, Nickel stopped off at home on the way to the darkroom to collect Miriam, but when he tried to slide his key into the building's front door, it wouldn't go.

"What are you doing there?" a voice yelled at him from inside the building. "What do you want?"

Nickel pressed his nose against the glass and peered in. Mr. Youdle was walking across the lobby toward him.

All at once, Nickel realized his mistake.

"Sorry!" he yelled through the glass. He turned and ran off down the street — down Ira Monk Street — his heart pounding. His head felt turned upside down. Inside out. He felt lost.

He stopped at 17th Street to get his bearings. If he was going home — his new home, the Beastly Arms — he was going in the wrong direction. The subway station, too, was behind him. Ahead was school, and Inez's building. He went ahead.

"Guess who's here to see you," Ms. Willamina said as she led Nickel into Inez's room.

Inez was propped up in bed again, reading one of the books he had brought her, Creatures of the Deep. There was a color photograph of a hammerhead shark on the front cover and a black-and-white squid on the back. Nickel noticed thin scabs crisscrossing the knuckles of Inez's hands. Aside from the top of her head, that was all of her he could see. The bandage was off. A small patch of her hair had been shaved to the scalp. Running down the center of this clearing was a line of stitches.

"Who?" she grunted behind her book.

Ms. Willamina didn't answer. She just folded her arms across her chest and waited for Inez to look for herself.

"Why, it's the space cadet!" Inez said, when she finally lowered her book. The bruises around her eyes had changed from purple to yellow. She was healing. And grinning.

Nickel grinned back.

"You be nice," Ms. Willamina said. "Nickel doesn't have to come all the way over here, you know. If he had any sense, he'd visit some other friend who's polite to him." She gave Inez a long look, then turned and walked from the room, going slow enough that Cecil, who was toddling along beside her, could keep up.

"That's right," Inez said, looking at Nickel. "He lives far away now. On another *planet*, almost!"

Nickel still smiled. He was glad she was more herself.

"How's Mr. Kirkaby?" Inez asked with an eyebrow raised.

"He went to dinner with us last night," Nickel said, sitting down on the edge of her bed.

Inez pretended to suppress a giggle. "So he's in love with your mama."

Nickel shrugged.

"I sure wouldn't want to eat dinner with my teacher!" Inez said, faking a shudder. "I don't think I'd be able to swallow!" She pretended to choke.

"It was all right," Nickel said. "Do you feel any different?" (He wanted to change the subject.) "Does your brain hurt or anything?"

"My *brain*?" Inez said, pulling her chin in. "Does my *brain* hurt? No! Does *yours*?" She crossed her eyes at him.

Nickel laughed awkwardly. "I mean, are you the same now? Is anything, I don't know, *different*?"

"Well," Inez said, tapping her chin with her finger and looking up at the ceiling. "I *do* see everything upside down now. And I never have to go to school again, or to the bathroom." She looked back down at him, pretending to be deadly serious. "And I can't say any words that have more than two syllables, of course. Other than that, I'm just the same as always."

Nickel stared at her, amazed. He didn't believe her, of course. He knew that the word "syllables" had three sylla-bles. He was just impressed that she could make all of that up on the spot.

"How's old Mr. Beastie?" Inez asked. "Tried to eat you yet?" She made a monster face and held up her hands like claws.

Nickel didn't bother to correct her. He knew she knew it was Beastly. "He sends his best wishes for a speedy re-covery." He looked down at the book in her lap. It was opened to a picture of a sea horse. "I took a picture last night."

"Really?" She pretended to be shocked. "A picture? You? What of? I can't imagine!"

"It wasn't clouds," Nickel said, smiling a bit. He en-joyed getting the chance to surprise her for once.

Inez's fake shocked expression turned into a slightly more genuine one. "No?" She leaned forward a little. "Then of what?"

"I don't know. The film's in the darkroom. I'll print it today."

Inez shook her head. "But what did you shoot at?"

Nickel shrugged. "Things," he said, his smile widening. "Things climbing down the wall of the Beastly Arms."

Inez raised both eyebrows. "*Things? What things?*"

"I told you, I don't know. It was dark. That's why I used Mom's flash."

"Why was it dark?" Inez asked.

"It was night. About two or so."

"In the *morning?*"

"I should be able to see what they were," Nickel went on, "if I focused right. They were definitely alive."

"Now, wait a minute," Inez said, closing her eyes and holding up her palm. "Are you trying to tell me there are living things crawling down the walls of your building?" She reopened her eyes and gave Nickel a very skeptical look.

He nodded.

Inez leaned forward. "I want to see this picture," she said.

19

"*WHERE'S* Miriam?" Gwendolyn asked as she passed the equipment Nickel had requested across the counter.

"At home," he answered. "I didn't have time to stop and get her."

"I understand," Gwendolyn said, nodding. "Busy, busy. It's a real rat race out there."

Nickel didn't even try to understand what that meant. It was probably another one of those adult things. He had more pressing matters on his mind.

His film was now plenty dry. He snipped off the long, black, unexposed section of it and tossed it into the trash, then switched on the light table and examined the negative with a magnifier. There was the wall, the windows, the vines. The things. They were still dark, but that was in negative. The blacks and whites were reversed. When he printed, they would be lighter. They looked furry. More than that he couldn't see. He'd have to enlarge it.

He mixed up his chemicals for printing, mounted the

negative into the negative carrier, slipped it into the enlarger head, switched off the overhead light, and switched on the enlarger lamp. The negative was projected onto the printing frame below. Nickel cranked the enlarger head up higher and the projected image outgrew the frame. He moved the frame so that one of the things was centered inside it, then he tested the focus with the magnifier. Normally at this point he did a test print to find the right exposure, but this time he was too impatient. He just took an educated guess (five seconds), set the timer, and flicked off the lamp. The room glowed red.

Next, he slid a sheet of photo paper into the frame, shiny side up, then hit the timer button. The lamp came back on. The thing, enlarged and in negative, was projected onto the paper. Five seconds later, the enlarger clicked off. Nickel removed the paper and carried it to the trays of chemicals. He slipped it into the soup first, tapping it under with rubber-tipped tongs. Within a few seconds an image began to appear. The thing was now five inches across, and, even under the red safelight, easier to make out.

It was an animal. It had fur, legs, a tail. Its tail was prehensile; it was clutching the vine. The flash of the strobe was reflected in the animal's dark eyes.

When the picture had finished developing, Nickel transferred it to the stop bath. Thirty seconds later, it went into the fix. Nickel counted to two hundred, then flicked on the overhead light. He lifted the print from the tray with the tongs, rinsed it in the print washer, then held it up to see. The image made him think of Alma.

"It's an opossum," he said.

Nickel went back to the enlarger and printed several blowups of the other dark forms on the wall. Some of them were opossums as well. There were also several shrews, a few rats, some mice, a couple of ferrets, a marten, and a spotted skunk. *That horrible smell*, Nickel thought. They were all climbing down the vines into the darkness below. Some were coming out of the windows.

Nickel put the prints in the print washer and watched them as they swirled around, trying to piece together what he was seeing. He assumed that all the animals had come from the windows. Where else could they have come from? Not the roof. He had been on the roof. Not the sky. Then Nickel wondered if maybe the bats had come from the windows as well. And the owl? He remembered the tenant who said, "Who?" He thought of the other noises he'd heard — the squeaking and the ruffling. He thought of how the building smelled like Miriam's box. He thought of the way that Mr. Beastly always looked at Miriam, how he'd known so much about kangaroo rats, how he'd seen the vampire bat cloud. He heard old voices, whispering in his head:

What your Mr. Youdle doesn't understand is that whether he's aware of it or not, all of his tenants are animals!

What is it — an apartment building for monsters?

"Not monsters," Nickel said to himself. "Beasts."

Nickel squeegeed the prints then laid them into his blotter book. He cleaned up the darkroom, checked in his equipment, then ran to the station and rode the train downtown. Like a mole.

He got off the train downtown, ran up 2nd Street to

Ira Monk Street, turned left, then left onto Tall Grass Drive. With his new key, he unlocked the sky blue door and ran through the foyer into the lobby. The plants were drooping again.

"Mr. Beastly!" he called out.

He waited for an answer, but when there was none, he ran up the stairs to the second floor. He smelled the kangaroo rat smell, but he heard nothing: no squeaking or ruffling, no "Who?" No Mr. Beastly.

"Mr. Beastly!" he called out again. He ran up to the third floor, then to the fourth, to the fifth. Each time, he stopped and called out, but there was never any answer.

The window at the end of the hall on the sixth floor wasn't shuttered. Through it, Nickel could see the shiny metal wall. He tiptoed down the hall, opened the window, and leaned out. Below was an open space as big as the playground at school. Bigger. It was overgrown with trees and bushes and plants. The smell of it — fresh and woodsy — filled his nostrils. He heard the sound of gurgling water and saw stars of light flickering through the greenery. Birds were flitting about in the treetops. He saw sparrows and finches and woodpeckers, pecking. An oriole flashed its sunny yellow plumage and then disappeared behind a canopy of leaves. A gray squirrel took over its place. Nickel leaned farther out the window. Above him, below him, to his right and left, were green vines. They covered the wall. There were no animals clinging to them.

"You called?" a voice said suddenly from behind him.

Nickel was so startled, he banged his head on the sash. When he turned around, he saw Mr. Beastly walking toward him down the hall. He was wearing his robe. Nickel gulped hard. A shiver crept up the back of his neck. He suddenly wondered if he'd been putting his nose where it didn't belong and whether he was just about to catch hell for it. When he thought of the pictures in the blotter book in his backpack, his fear tripled.

Mr. Beastly stopped a few feet from him. He looked over Nickel's shoulder at the opened window. "Doing a little snooping?" he said.

"I-I'm sorry," Nickel said. His heart pounded in his throat.

"For what, son?" Mr. Beastly said. "It's no crime to look out a window." He turned and headed back the way he'd come. "Close it, please, then follow me," he said over his shoulder.

Nickel stayed where he was, watching Mr. Beastly as he walked away down the hall. He felt a strong urge to make a run for it, but Mr. Beastly was between him and the stairs. He turned and looked out the window.

"Come on, now," Mr. Beastly called out. "I have things I want to show you."

Nickel's urge to flee suddenly left him. Somehow he knew that Mr. Beastly meant him no harm. He could feel it in his stomach. He pulled the window shut.

"I t-took some p-p-pictures," he said, looking down at the floor.

Mr. Beastly stopped. He turned around. He was smiling. "I know," he said. "Never mind about that." He held out a pair of latex gloves and a white mask. "Come here. Put these on."

Nickel did as he was told without even stopping to

wonder why. Then, when Mr. Beastly had put on his own mask and gloves, he opened the door to apartment 6B. A strong, musty odor rushed out.

"Come inside," he whispered through his mask. "I want you to see."

The only light in the room came from the door to the hall. The windowpanes were painted black. The floor was covered with dirt. Plants were growing up out of it, weeds, mostly, but also some grass, a few flowers, some vines. In the large room ahead of him — the living room — two rotted logs were lying in the dirt in a V shape. A row of insects crawled along the top of one.

Mr. Beastly stepped past him. "This way," he whispered to Nickel.

Nickel followed without thinking. His brain was busy processing all that his eyes and ears and nose were sending it. As he neared the logs, he saw that the insects were ants. He felt an urge to roll one of the logs over with his foot. He'd read many times about all the things that often live underneath.

"Take a look there," Mr. Beastly whispered very quietly, pointing down at the other side of the log.

Nickel stepped quietly around. A low, wheezing sound, a snore, rose up from the darkness. It was as repetitive as a clock. Nickel leaned forward, squinting, trying to see what was there, but the other log was casting a shadow over it. He crouched down and shielded the light from the hall with his hand. It was still too dark. He took a deep breath. He had to be patient, had to let his eyes adjust to the darkness.

Soon he could make out an outline, then, a bit later, fur, then whiskers, then an ear. The animal was a good size, about as big as a large house cat. When Nickel's eyes had adjusted more, he could make out two paws folded under a chin. The snout was white. There was a black stripe — a mask — over the eyes.

Nickel looked up at Mr. Beastly. "It's a raccoon," he whispered.

Mr. Beastly just smiled.

Nickel looked back down at it, watched it breathe in and out, its head rocking slightly as it did. Its nose was black and seemed to be working — sniffing — even as the animal slept. Its paws had long, black fingers. Nickel read once that a raccoon could turn doorknobs, even open refrigerator doors, in its quest for food. Its fur looked stiff and coarse, not soft like a cat's. Nickel remembered touching the raccoon in the gutter.

After a few minutes had gone by, Mr. Beastly touched Nickel on the shoulder and then tiptoed away toward the door. Nickel reluctantly left the raccoon behind and followed along. As he crossed the room, he noticed a maze of large metal ducts above him on the ceiling. Off in the corner, several of them ran down into the floor.

When Nickel stepped back out into the hall, Mr. Beastly pulled the door shut behind him. The two of them stood silently, smiling a while, then Nickel peered down the hall at the rows of doors. The hair on the back of his neck bristled as he thought about what might be behind them.

Mr. Beastly chuckled to himself. "Why don't we drop in next door and say hello?" he said. He walked down to 6D, and turned the doorknob, and the door opened. "I never lock them."

"What about the raccoon?" Nickel asked. " Couldn't it let itself out?"

Mr. Beastly laughed. "I guess he could, but, for whatever reason, he never has. Maybe it hasn't occurred to him. You won't mention it to him, will you?"

Nickel shook his head seriously.

"Good lad," Mr. Beastly said. "Come on now."

6D was much the same as 6B: blackened windowpanes, earthen floor, underbrush. But in the living room, instead of logs, there was a mound. It was about as tall as Nickel's knee and was made of mud and twigs and leaves and string and bottle caps and lots of other stuff. Nickel knew just what it was — a midden — and he felt pretty sure about what had made it: a pack rat.

"Do you know what lives in there?" Mr. Beastly whispered into Nickel's ear.

Nickel nodded.

Mr. Beastly patted his head. "I thought so," he whispered. "I was right about you."

○   ○   ○

Mr. Beastly opened all the doors of all the rooms on all the floors, from the sixth to the ninth. Nickel saw jumping mice and pocket mice and grasshopper mice; he saw voles, shrews, ferrets, gophers, and moles. In 6F, there was a gray fox sleeping in a dead tree stump; in 7C, there was an opossum family, the babies sleeping on their mother's back; in 7F, a prickly porcupine; in 8E, a badger, dug into the floor. It snarled ever so slightly, and Nickel backed off; he'd read how fierce they could be. The rooms on the ninth floor were filled with all sorts of bats — silver-haired, Mexican free-tailed, mouse-eared. There were hundreds of them! They hung upside down from the moldings, from light fixtures, from curtain rods and towel racks. They looked like little closed-up umbrellas.

"Their droppings make excellent fertilizer," Mr. Beastly said as he closed the door to 9G.

Then he led Nickel up the final flight of stairs, to the roof. Nickel had never been up there during the day. The sky was filled with clouds, but Nickel barely noticed them. There were plenty of real animals to see. They walked to the edge of the building and looked down at the open space below. It was green and lush. Birds were singing in the trees and beasts were rustling in the undergrowth.

Nickel looked up at Mr. Beastly.

"Sure," Mr. Beastly said. "This way."

They started back down the stairs.

"What are all the ducts for?" Nickel asked as they descended.

Mr. Beastly smiled. "I bet you can figure it out," he said.

Nickel thought for a second. There hadn't been ducts in all of the rooms. There hadn't been any, for example, in the bats' room. The ducts didn't seem to open up into vents so he doubted that they were for heating or cooling or ventilation. They came down out of the ceiling and ran down into the floor.

"Tunnels?" Nickel said.

Mr. Beastly laughed. "You are a remarkable boy, Nicholas Dill!" he said.

Nickel felt his face tingle with pride.

"And I suppose you've already deduced who uses the tunnels, right?" Mr. Beastly said.

Nickel shrugged. "Burrowers?" he said.

Mr. Beastly smiled. "For example?"

"Gophers," Nickel said, thinking. "Voles. The badger?"

Mr. Beastly nodded. "The tunnels are filled with earth. Some are big; some are small. The badgers use the big ones."

"Where do the tunnels go?" Nickel asked.

Mr. Beastly looked down at him, smiling, waiting.

"Outside?" Nickel asked.

"You are quite the detective," Mr. Beastly said. "Yes. Outside to the wood. I'll show you."

They climbed the stairs all the way down to the first floor. Nickel had only seen the foyer and the lobby and had mistakenly assumed that that was all there was. He was quite surprised and delighted when Mr. Beastly pushed a spot on the wall in the lobby and a small, square panel — a little smaller than a developing tray — popped open. Inside of it was a doorknob. Mr. Beastly turned it and a small, square door opened up. It was only as tall as

Nickel's shoulders. He would never have guessed it was there.

"This way," Mr. Beastly said. "There are steps. Careful."

He bent over and passed through the little doorway. Nickel followed him inside. There were wooden stairs going down. Nickel stopped on the first one. Mr. Beastly reached past him and pulled the door closed.

Wherever they were, it was pitch black. Nickel couldn't even see Mr. Beastly standing beside him. He couldn't see his own hand in front of his face.

Maybe it's a darkroom, Nickel thought.

"Let's let our eyes adjust a minute," Mr. Beastly said quietly. "I know it's dark now, but you'll see better soon enough."

Nickel smiled. It pleased him to hear Mr. Beastly say aloud the words he had so often heard in his own head. Hearing them in the darkness like that almost made it seem that it was not Mr. Beastly at all. It sounded like the voice of Nickel's own mind speaking.

As Nickel waited, he noticed a deep rumbling, like a

furnace, coming from somewhere. And he smelled laun-
dry. It smelled hot and clean and dry.

He could hear Mr. Beastly breathing. It had a slight rasp
to it — a wheeze. For the second time, Nickel wondered
how old he was. Nickel wasn't very good at guessing the
age of adults. *Is he sixty?* he thought. *Seventy? A hundred?* He
couldn't tell. He looked in the direction of Mr. Beastly's
voice. He could now see a vague outline of him.

"The furnaces are down here," Mr. Beastly said. "And
the washing machines. The lights went out a while ago
and I keep meaning to fix them but I never seem to find
the time. Better to light a candle than to curse the darkness, they say." He laughed. "I never curse the darkness.
I've learned a lot from it." He paused a moment, then
added, "I can see well enough now. How about you?"

"I guess so," Nickel said.

"There are fifteen stairs, no landing," Mr. Beastly said.
"Hang onto the handrail and you'll be all right. Then it's
just straight down the hall. Follow my footsteps."

Nickel did as Mr. Beastly said. He went down the steps,

then walked along the hall, listening intently to the padding of Mr. Beastly's bare feet on the cement floor ahead of him. At one point the sound of his footsteps changed. They sounded as if they were walking on wood and they sounded heavier. And then suddenly Nickel heard a metal latch slide open and a rectangle of bright light lit up the hallway from above. It was so sudden and so bright that Nickel shielded his eyes.

"Up here, son," Mr. Beastly said.

Nickel lowered his arm, squinting in the light.

It's just as hard to adjust to the light, he thought.

He inched forward into it. As he got closer, he saw that there was another staircase — also wooden — and that the door to the outside was at the top of it. When he looked up at the door, he had to shield his eyes again.

Mr. Beastly laughed. "You could just as well curse the light!"

When Nickel reached the bottom stair he found the handrail and pulled himself up. Fifteen steps later he reached the door, and looked out onto a dense green world of living things.

"Welcome to Sullivan Wood!" Mr. Beastly announced, then added out of the corner of his mouth, "Or what's left of it anyway."

Nickel wandered out, careful where he stepped, his eyes, his ears — all his senses — working hard, gathering information. There were several tall trees. Some had needles and pinecones; others had leaves and acorns. The smell reminded him of Christmas. Nickel saw more than a few nests in their branches; he heard twittering and pecking and squawking. Butterflies and bees and bugs floated through the air, buzzing or whizzing or making no sound at all, then settling down upon the flowers and the bushes. Fallen needles and leaves were scattered across the forest floor, as were acorns and pinecones, berries and blossoms, scat, and, under one tree, an owl pellet. Nickel looked up and spotted a great horned owl sleeping in the crook of two branches. It looked like a cat.

On the ground, Nickel also found openings to tunnels and burrows, and mounds of loose soil. Around a mud puddle, Nickel spied prints — four-toed, three-toed, hooved. As he examined them, a black king snake slithered past his foot. Further on, in a clearing, was a watering hole. *A white-tailed deer was drinking from it!* Nickel didn't breathe. He watched as the deer raised its head on its long brown neck. Its eyes were bigger and blacker than any photograph would have led him to believe were possible. They looked directly at him. Nickel stared back, frozen to the spot. Then, suddenly, the deer turned and, with one mighty leap, vanished into the brush.

This is it! Nickel thought. *This is the secret!*

But he knew there had to be more to it than that. He thought of Mr. Kirkaby's interview instructions. It's not enough to find out what; you have to find out why. Why were the animals here? Why weren't there people? Why was Mr. Beastly here? Why had he allowed Nickel — and his mom — here? And why was Mr. Beastly keeping this secret in the first place?

Nickel turned and looked back at Mr. Beastly. He was still standing by the open door. *All the answers are inside him,* Nickel thought.

"I have to go," Mr. Beastly said. "I have a lot to do." He

turned to leave, then said over his shoulder, "Close the door when you come in, okay?"

Nickel smiled. Mr. Beastly trusted him. He would have loved to go with him, to help him with whatever it was that needed doing, but he said, "Okay." Mr. Beastly disappeared into the building. The last thing Nickel saw of him was the bottom of a muddy foot.

When Nickel turned back, he saw a kangaroo rat on the ground amid the pine needles, gnawing on an acorn. It was Miriam. He hadn't noticed she'd left his pocket. His first thought was to scoop her up. He didn't want anything to eat her. But then he decided to leave her be.

She can take care of herself, he thought.

Nickel took a deep breath, inhaling the sweet smell of pine and wildflowers, then moved mindfully into the tangle, careful of where his feet fell. There was no easy going — no road, no sidewalk, no path. The wood wasn't like the park. It was a mess. A wonderful mess.

And then, before Nickel knew it, the sun began to set behind the building tops and the clouds began turning orange. Nickel spent the golden hour in Sullivan Wood, watching a trap-door spider spinning a web in a hole in the ground, watching a gray squirrel gathering nuts and storing them in a hole in a tree, watching an ant lion lying in wait for prey, watching the grass grow. Never had Nickel wished so much that the night would wait. But it came, right on schedule. He stayed in the wood until it was dark, then he collected Miriam (and a few acorns) and began wending his way back to the door. When he reached it, he turned back and listened. The buzz of insects grew louder. The birds were quiet. And then, from above, Nickel heard windows opening. A moment later, he saw small dark forms shimmying down the vines.

He opened the door and stepped inside, leaving the forest to the creatures of the night.

20

"SO how did your pictures come out?" Nickel's mom asked at the dinner table that night.

Nickel plucked a sesame seed out of his salad and dropped it into his pocket for Miriam. "Okay," he said.

"Can I see them after dinner?"

Nickel shrugged. He hadn't made up his mind yet about telling his mom what he'd seen. Maybe Mr. Beastly wanted him to keep it to himself. *Sometimes people keep things to themselves for good reasons,* he heard Mr. Kirkaby say.

"Which animals did you see this time?" his mom asked with a grin.

Nickel smiled. "A raccoon in a log. A trap door spider. A king snake. A white-tailed —"

He was interrupted by a knock on the door.

"Who could that be?" his mom whispered. "I didn't buzz anyone in." She stood up and started toward the door. "It must be one of the other tenants."

Nickel imagined a badger knocking on the front door and had to suppress a snicker.

"Good evening, Mrs. Wilde," he heard Mr. Beastly say. "I hope I'm not disturbing you."

Nickel jumped up and ran toward the foyer. Mr. Beastly was standing in the doorway in his suit and tie.

"No. Come on in," Nickel's mom said. "And please call me Maud."

"Thank you, Maud," Mr. Beastly said, stepping inside. "Good evening, Nicholas," he said, and gave him a wink.

Nickel smiled. The wink said a lot. He knew now why Mr. Beastly had come. He wouldn't have to tell his mom after all.

"Have a seat," Nickel's mom said, leading him into the living room.

Mr. Beastly sat down on the couch. Nickel's mom sat beside him. Nickel sat on the daybed, formerly his bed. He still had his napkin in his collar.

"So?" his mom said.

"I have a few things I would like to discuss with you," Mr. Beastly said. "About the building." He shifted in his seat. "About the smell."

Nickel's mom relaxed a little. She had been sitting

rather rigidly, waiting for Mr. Beastly to get to the point of his visit, and now she thought he had.

"Yes," she said. "It's very . . . well . . . *strong.*"

Mr. Beastly nodded. "Yes, I'm very sorry about that. I wish there was something I could do about it."

Nickel's mom's spine stiffened. Her brow wrinkled. "You can't do anything about it?" she said.

"I'm afraid not," Mr. Beastly said. He shot Nickel a nervous glance, and Nickel nodded his encouragement.

"I hope you'll understand," Mr. Beastly went on. "I really wouldn't want you to move away —"

"Move away! Why would we have to do that? Is it dangerous? What is it?"

"No, no," Mr. Beastly said, shaking his head. "It's not like that. There's no danger. "It's just, well . . . it's . . ."

He looked at Nickel again. "Go on," Nickel mouthed.

"Well, let me ask you this, Maud," Mr. Beastly said, twiddling his tie. "How do you feel about — *animals?*"

"I *thought* it was an animal!" Nickel's mom said. "Did someone's pet die or something?"

"No," Mr. Beastly said. "That's just it. None of the other tenants *have* pets."

Nickel's mom glanced at Nickel's shirt pocket. Then she looked back at Mr. Beastly. "But you said it was all right," she said. "You saw his kangaroo rat and you said it was all right —"

"No, no, no," Mr. Beastly said, waving his palm up at her. "I'm not making myself clear. Of course, Miriam is welcome here. All animals are welcome here. That's exactly what I'm trying to say."

Nickel's mom closed her eyes and shook her head. "I guess I just don't get it," she sighed.

Mr. Beastly looked over at Nickel and made a gesture with his head — a quick tilt of it toward Nickel's mom. It seemed to mean, "I can't do it. You'll have to tell her." Nickel pointed at his chest and said, aloud, "*Me?*"

"What?" his mom said, opening her eyes.

She looked over at him with a confused expression. Then she turned back to Mr. Beastly. His face blushed. She looked back at Nickel.

"Do you know what this is about?" she asked.

He blushed, too, suddenly feeling very guilty for not having already told her.

"Well, do you?" his mom pressed.

"Mom," Nickel said. "The tenants *are* animals."

"Exactly!" Mr. Beastly said.

Nickel's mom looked over at Mr. Beastly, then back at Nickel, then back at Mr. Beastly. A smile gradually appeared on her face. She brought her hands up and clapped them together.

"Oh!" she said. "I get it! I remember! Mr. Youdle! 'All of his tenants are animals!' 'His building is full of animals!'"

She laughed. Very hard. It was infectious. Mr. Beastly began to laugh, too. Then Nickel. They all rocked with laughter.

Then Nickel's mom abruptly stopped. "So, now," she said soberly. "What's this all about *really*?" She folded her hands in her lap.

Mr. Beastly rose to his feet. "I think it'd be best if I just showed you," he said.

Nickel jumped up from the daybed, eager to see the tenants again. His mom stayed seated on the couch.

"Show me *what?*" she said. Nickel could tell she was no longer fooling around.

"The *tenants*, Mom," Nickel said.

"Yes!" Mr. Beastly said. "That's it! I want to introduce you to some of the tenants! They can explain things much better than I can!" He held his hand out toward her.

She took it and let him pull her to her feet. "O-Okay," she said, confused again. "Which ones?"

"Why don't we start across the hall," Mr. Beastly said. "With the foxes."

"The Foxes," Nickel's mom said. "They can explain about the smell?"

"Yes," Mr. Beastly said, leading her to the door. "You'll understand much better after you've met them."

"Explain!" Nickel's mom demanded in the hall outside the foxes' apartment. Her eyes were open wider than Nickel had ever seen them. "I want it straight and I want it now! *What's going on in this building!*"

Mr. Beastly tugged at his tie. "It's complicated," he said.

Nickel's mom glared at him. Her posture was so stiff, a sudden breeze might have snapped her in two. "Try anyway," she said.

"Yes, yes," Mr. Beastly said, pacing back and forth. "I'm trying to think of where to begin."

Nickel's mom tapped her foot impatiently, her arms crossed. Nickel stood beside her, leaning forward slightly, eager to hear what Mr. Beastly had to say. Miriam trembled feverishly in his pocket. She hadn't enjoyed meeting the foxes.

"The first thing you must understand is that you are in no danger," Mr. Beastly said. "I've lived here for forty years with little more than an occasional scratch."

"Those were *foxes!*" Nickel's mom said suddenly. "Real *foxes!*"

"Yes," Mr. Beastly said. "Red foxes."

"*What are they doing in that apartment?*"

"Well, they live there. At least, during the day they do. They'll be heading out soon, looking for food."

Nickel's mom shook her head. "They live here? In the *building?*"

Mr. Beastly nodded. "They're good tenants. Very neat. Quiet."

"What about the other rooms?" she asked.

"Well, on this floor, next to the foxes — in 2B — there's a family of shrews," he said, "and in 2A there are a few different rats and mice — some woodrats, house mice, a couple of grasshopper mice. Down in 2H, there are some gophers — pocket gophers, to be exact. Apartment 2G has ferrets and weasels, and down in 2D, there's a barn owl. A big one."

The one that says 'Who?' Nickel thought with a smile. He wondered if it was the same one he'd seen the other night, or if there were more than one. He realized he hadn't seen all the rooms yet, or all the tenants. He'd only seen the rooms above the fifth floor. *I can't wait to see the rest!* he thought.

Nickel's mom walked very slowly — like a loris — up to Mr. Beastly. He stopped pacing. "What about *people?*" she asked. "Aren't there any *people* in this building?"

Mr. Beastly grinned wryly. "Just us," he said.

Nickel's mom was not amused. She took a step closer.

Not a foot separated the two of them. "You mean to tell me that, except for the three of us, everyone that lives here is an *animal*?"

"Mom," Nickel interrupted. "We're animals, too."

"He's right," Mr. Beastly said timidly, taking a step backward. "We are."

"You know what I mean!" Nickel's mom yelled.

"Y-Yes, yes, I do," Mr. Beastly said, recoiling. "Please, Maud. Let me explain."

"Oh, I *knew* this was too good to be true!" she sighed. "I *knew* there was something, something . . . I don't know . . . fishy. But how could I have guessed *this!*"

A long, faint squeal punctuated her sentence. Miriam chirped a response.

"That's a grasshopper mouse," Mr. Beastly said.

"They howl," Nickel added.

"That was a *howl*?" Nickel's mom said. "It sounded more like an electronic flash warming up."

"Well, they have such tiny lungs," Mr. Beastly said with a grin.

The mouse howled again and they all stood still, listening. Then Miriam scrambled out of Nickel's pocket to his shoulder and sniffed the air.

"She sure seems right at home," Mr. Beastly said, smiling at her.

Nickel peeked down at her and nodded.

"That's as may be," his mom said. "But I need some questions answered before I can settle into a . . . a . . . zoo!"

"Oh, no," Mr. Beastly said. "Not a zoo. Not at all. I'd better explain. But not here. Follow me. I know a better place."

21

MR. BEASTLY pushed the door open and they all stepped out onto the roof. A nearly full moon was rising up over the skyline in the east and reflecting a soft, warm light over the rooftops. The stars twinkled in a clear sky, but Nickel didn't connect them. He was busy concentrating on Mr. Beastly, wanting desperately to hear the rest of the secret — the why. Miriam, however, showed no such interest. She immediately climbed down to the cement and began searching for food, keeping one eye on the lookout for owls.

Mr. Beastly walked to the ledge and stood staring out over Sullivan Wood and the city. Nickel and his mom joined him there.

"Pretty," Nickel's mom said softly.

Mr. Beastly nodded, then took a deep breath and began.

"When I was a young man, I was an architect for a big firm. There were a lot of buildings going up, so I was very busy. I designed many of the building in this neighbor-hood, in fact. I worked on the post office over on Jacquet, and the library on Hennessy."

That's one of mine, Nickel remembered Mr. Beastly saying of the Rialto. He thought about the light streaming down from the dome in the library's central hall. Mr. Beastly had designed that dome. *They're all mine,* Nickel heard him say-ing. *Or rather, they all own me.*

"I was happy. I had lots of money. A nice car. Big fins in the back." He smiled. "I was young. What did I know?" His expression darkened. "But then, one day, when I was out on a site, something happened.

"The workers were breaking ground for a new sky-scraper. They were boring a hole with a huge drill. They'd dug maybe ten or fifteen feet down and were just about to pour cement in, when I heard something." He cocked his ear as if he were hearing it again. "I have no idea how I heard anything over all that noise, but I did. It was a cry — a high-pitched cry. It sounded like it was coming from the hole. So I went over to have a look. The crew was yelling at me to get out of the way. They wanted to pour their cement, and I was standing in front of the chute." He laughed to himself.

"It was too dark in the hole to see, so I called the foreman over and borrowed his flashlight. But I still couldn't see anything. So, finally, they made me move away. Then the foreman yelled 'Let her go!' and that cement came sliding down the chute, wet and gray and heavy. I watched it pour, still feeling in my bones that something wasn't right, when suddenly, just before the cement reached the end, I saw something poke its head out of the hole! It was an animal! At the time I didn't know what kind. It was gray and velvety-looking and had a long pink nose and big pink claws. It didn't seem to have any eyes."

"A mole?" Nickel asked.

"Yes," Mr. Beastly said, looking down at Nickel. "A hairy-tailed, I imagine."

"So what happened?" Nickel's mom asked.

"I yelled for them to stop, but no one could hear me over the noise. I doubt it would've mattered anyway. The next second that cement dropped onto the poor thing's head. Pushed it back down the hole. Covered it over." Mr. Beastly stopped a minute. A chirp rose up from the wood below. "I stood there hoping it would be all right, hoping it would dig itself free. But then they sank in the beam . . ." He paused. "A twenty-foot steel I-beam. I couldn't see how . . ."

His eyes lowered. Nickel's mom shook her head. Nickel fought away a horrible image — of the mole and the beam — that flashed before his mind's eye.

"From then on," Mr. Beastly said, "I spent a lot more time on the sites. Every day if I could. The workers weren't always so appreciative. I suppose architects make builders nervous." He smiled.

"The first animal I rescued was a chipmunk. It was in a deep wheel track. A second later and a tractor would have backed right over it. I scooped it up in a can and took it home. I bought it a cage, gave it a name: Walter. She had a litter a couple of days later. I got a few more cages. I didn't know anything about chipmunks so I went to the library and checked out a few books. Before too long I had added a few mice, a couple of bats, some lizards and snakes, and a whole lot of earthworms and bugs and such. My apartment was stacked with cages, boxes, books — I had to check out quite a few more."

"Why didn't you take the animals out to the country and set them free?" Nickel's mom asked.

Nickel wondered the same thing, but didn't ask. That's not what he'd done when he'd found Miriam.

"I thought about that, but somehow it didn't seem right. I didn't know if they'd survive out there. I'd read that animals usually belong to a very specific habitat, and that randomly plopping them into another one could be fatal — and not just for them, but for the other animals already living there as well. It seemed to me that, since I'd saved them, I had to house them, and feed them. They were my responsibility."

They owned him, Nickel thought.

"I was bringing home at least one new creature every week, and some of them were reproducing. It was getting to be a problem — at home, I mean. I didn't live with anyone. I didn't have a family. It wasn't that. It was just that

I lived in a one-bedroom apartment and the animals were taking over."

"You didn't have any family?" Nickel asked. "Not even a mom?"

Mr. Beastly smiled. "We all have moms," he said. "She lived in New Hampshire then. What I mean is that I had no wife, no children. I never married. I didn't intend it to be that way. I was just too busy with the animals. As I said, they were quite a handful.

"At some point I decided to convert the bedroom into a home for them. A kind of habitat. I didn't have a problem with moving my bed into the living room. I didn't want the gnawers to get into other parts of the apartment, or, worse, into other peoples' apartments! So I installed some clear polyacrylic on the floor and the walls. Then I brought in bag after bag of potting soil and poured it on top. I gathered whatever plants and stones from the building sites as I could without drawing too much attention to myself. I kept experimenting with different plants. I brought in mulch and dead leaves and more bugs, especially worms. They helped out quite a bit, keeping things turned.

"A lot of the plants died. So did a lot of the animals. Some ate each other, but most of them were herbivorous. I didn't lose any species — just individuals. Eventually, it all balanced out. Settled down. I ended up with a little food chain in my bedroom!"

"But what about the smell?" Nickel asked. "Didn't it stink?"

"That I couldn't do anything about," Mr. Beastly said. "I tried everything: sprays and scented candles and those pop-up room deodorizers. Nothing worked." He looked at Nickel's mom. "I still haven't solved that problem."

"Obviously," she said.

"But that wasn't the only thing," he went on. "The animals were noisy, too — chattering and scratching — especially at night when the building was quiet. Tenants starting showing up at my door, telling me to keep my dog quiet, or my cat. All it would take was one surprise inspection by the landlord and then all the animals would be out on the street, myself included. I had to think of something else.

"At the time, I was working on this building — the

Beastly Arms — though that wasn't its intended name. I don't remember what they were planning to call it. It was going to be a skyscraper, the tallest in the city. That was what the client wanted. He wanted to be able to look down on everybody, I suppose. Anyway, before we came in and started tearing everything up, there was a wood here, Sullivan Wood. It was a real forest — not a city park. The original city planners had done their level best to ensure that it would always be a wilderness park, but the best laid plans of mice and men, and all that. We cut it down — most of it, anyway. My menagerie grew daily during this time. That was when I adopted my first gray fox. She was my first real predator and had quite an effect on the rodent population. I can't say I was exactly sorry." He looked down at Miriam, who was sniffing around by his feet. "No offense, Miriam, but rodents do get out of hand without predators around."

Miriam poked her head up at the sound of her name, then resumed her hunt.

"Then one day I looked around at what was going on in my apartment, and what was happening to Sullivan

Wood, and I had a brainstorm. The next day I walked into the client's office and made him an offer on the place. He just laughed. So I offered more. Then I waived my architect's fee. As I said, I'd been doing very well. I lived very simply. I wasn't one to go out on the town. The habitat left me no time for friends, and I had no expensive habits — no art collections, no silk suits, no racehorses. I realized I had quite a lot of money just lying around. So I offered the client *twice* the amount the building was costing him. He had to give in to that. He just built his tower somewhere else.

"Naturally, everyone thought I was crazy. The firm fired me. But I didn't care. I left my apartment and moved myself and my roommates in here. I called it the Beastly Arms as kind of a joke." He snickered. "My name is actually Beasley. I thought Beastly was funny. Later, I started using the name.

"I cancelled all the orders for the building, all the refrigerators and dishwashers and toilets and tubs. I sent all the contractors away, all the workers — except for the roofers. I told them to build the roof on the building right away. It was nine floors high at the time. Meanwhile, I worked on the inside, laying polyacrylic on the floors, walls, and, this time, the ceilings. I brought in dirt, installed ductwork so the burrowing animals — the gophers and moles and such — could get in and out. I planted vines outside that reached up to the windows. I landscaped the rooms. It was a full-time job.

"When the roofers were finished, I let the animals out. If they'd wanted to, they could have left. The wood wasn't enclosed. But most of them stayed. Within a day or two they had set up their territories. A lot of the nocturnal animals preferred to stay indoors during the day. The climbers could use the vines, the burrowers, the ducts. The fliers used the windows. I opened them each evening to let them out and each morning to let them back in."

Nickel remembered the sound he'd heard — shhh-THUNK! — just before the bats flew up at him the other night on the roof. It was the sound of a window sliding open.

"I lost quite a few animals in the beginning. I found a

few of them from time to time out on the street, run down by cars. Others just disappeared. Even still, the population kept growing. I wasn't bringing in any new animals, but those already here were reproducing at a healthy clip. I converted one room after another into habitats. All the rooms are converted now — except yours, of course — and I could use more! Seventy-three rooms and I need more room!"

"And no one's ever suspected?" Nickel's mom asked. "No one's ever seen anything? *Smelled* anything?"

"No one's ever complained," Mr. Beastly said with a shrug. "It helps that there are no windows on the neighboring buildings. As you can see, two of them are warehouses." He pointed at the building to the right and the metal one straight ahead. "That one used to be an apartment building, but since it was built right up against the Beastly Arms, there were no windows to worry about." He pointed to the red-brick building to the left. "Now, of course, it's condemned. It's caving in inside. It was just dumb luck, really. These three buildings have protected us. They've formed a barricade around us against the city — kept us safely hidden inside. And they've preserved Sullivan Wood." He nodded down at it. "What's left of it."

"That's the forest?" Nickel's mom said.

"Can we show her?" Nickel asked.

"In the morning," Mr. Beastly said, rubbing Nickel's hair. "If she wants to."

"Wait till you see, Mom! It's *so* great!"

"Well, what about diseases?" his mom asked Mr. Beastly. "Rabies. Viruses. Don't you get sick?"

"I've been lucky," Mr. Beastly said. "Most of the animals don't venture out, so they don't get exposed to anything. I always figured the bats would be the likeliest to bring something in, but if they have, I've never seen it. There's never been a rabid animal here. As far as other diseases — viruses and parasites and such — I just do my best to protect myself. I keep the animals in their rooms when they're in the building. The rooms are quite secure. I've never seen anything bigger than a spider in my quarters or in the halls. I always wear a mask and gloves around the tenants, and I never actually come into physical contact with them. I stay away from their scat and their urine. I do my best to avoid becoming a nuisance, and that keeps me out of trouble, I think."

"How did the deer get here?" Nickel asked.

"*Deer?*" his mom said.

"There's one in the woods," Mr. Beastly said. "I was driving one night out in the country, and, sadly, I hit it. He was just a fawn then. I brought him here and nursed him back to health. That was a long time ago." He looked at Nickel. "That was the last time I was ever in a car."

"Did you ever go back to work?" Nickel's mom asked.

"Once everything here settled down I did, but just for a short time. I had to quit after a while. This place was taking up more and more of my time. I was able to put some money away, though. The building was paid for. All I needed money for was to pay taxes and such. Only I use the gas and electricity — and now you. The other tenants don't need them. The property taxes are pretty cheap, too. It's not the neighborhood it used to be. As for myself, I don't need much. It's surprising how little one really needs."

"You mean you've lived here with just the animals your whole life?" Nickel asked.

Mr. Beastly looked down at him, his brow furrowed. "Well, not my *whole* life," he said.

"Your whole *adult* life though?" Nickel's mom asked.

"I suppose so," Mr. Beastly said, looking away.

"You don't have any friends?" Nickel asked. He thought of Inez, how unhappy he'd be without her.

"I didn't plan it that way," Mr. Beastly said. "That's just the way things turned out."

"But haven't you been lonely?" Nickel's mom asked.

Mr. Beastly blinked and his eyes grew misty. They glimmered in the moon's light. "I've stayed busy," he said. "Busy enough not to really notice."

"But *why*?" Nickel's mom asked. "Why did you do it all alone?"

"I'm responsible," Mr. Beastly said, looking out at the rooftops. "It's my duty to take care of things."

"But you didn't have to do it all alone," Nickel's mom said. "People aren't all bad, you know. You could have asked for help."

"Yes," Mr. Beastly said very quietly, "I could have."

"I'll help," Nickel said almost as quietly. "If you want me to."

Mr. Beastly smiled at him and a few tears ran down into the creases of his face. "Yes," he said. "I'd like that."

Just then, Miriam let out a loud squeak and scrambled up Nickel's pant leg to his shirt. She dove into his pocket and made herself as small as possible.

Before Nickel could say "What is it?" a shadow flickered past the moon, and he saw the barn owl wheeling overhead, its claws tucked against its feathery belly.

"Look at that!" his mom gasped.

Mr. Beastly smiled. "Maud," he said, "I'd like you to meet your neighbor, from 2D!"

22

NICKEL'S mom agreed to stay in the building. She wouldn't guarantee they would stay permanently. She wanted to see how things went, whether or not she could get used to the smell, whether or not she could, as she put it, "get used to the idea of living in a building full of critters."

"I realize that in this town, you have to be willing to overlook minor annoyances if you want a nice, affordable place to live," she told Mr. Beastly. "Let's face it: I've lived with rodents before, and I'm not referring to Mr. Youdle, either. Besides, I've been saying to Nickel for years that I'd move us out to the country, and I guess this is about as close as we can get without actually having to leave the city!"

To avoid Nickel's dad discovering the truth about the Beastly Arms, Nickel began taking the train to Oak Hollow on his dad's Sundays. Nickel wondered why his dad never took the train to the city during the week instead of sitting in bumper-to-bumper traffic and paying to park in a garage. But he didn't ask. His dad was an adult and probably had his reasons.

Meanwhile, Mr. Beastly showed Nickel the rest of the rooms and taught him the workings of the building: how to check the ducts, how to seal cracks and rusted spots, how to check for rotting or gnawed wood; what and when to water, where the best places to catch bugs and earthworms were and when and how to put them into the rooms; and, most important, what to leave alone.

"The idea," Mr. Beastly said, "is to let the elements take hold, but to keep them from bringing down the house."

Nickel helped Mr. Beastly move all the plants from the lobby back up to the rooms they'd come from. Mr. Beastly had only moved them downstairs for show, to "smarten the place up a bit for your mom," he said. That was why they kept wilting; they had been recently transplanted and hadn't taken to the new room very well. That and the fact that Mr. Beastly kept forgetting to water them.

He gave Nickel floor plans that noted, in general,

which species lived in which rooms and how many of each of them he thought there were and an approximate schedule of when Nickel could expect them to be awake or asleep. Of course, it was all subject to change.

"They don't read floor plans or wear watches," Mr. Beastly said.

Nowhere on the floor plan did it indicate where Mr. Beastly's room was, but it wasn't difficult for Nickel to figure it out. It had to be in the basement, along the dark corridor leading to the wood. There was a room down there that wasn't marked on the floor plan, and it was the only room in the building Nickel hadn't been in.

Then one day, as Nickel was feeling his way down through the corridor — Mr. Beastly never did fix the lights — the door to this room suddenly opened. The light from inside made Nickel wince.

"You found me," Mr. Beastly said. "I knew it wouldn't take you long. I'd invite you in but the place is such a mess."

Apparently, he never did clean it up, because he never got around to asking Nickel, or his mom, in.

"Maybe he's just a private person," his mom said. "We should just respect that."

Nickel nodded. "Okay," he said. But he wanted to see inside the apartment just the same.

Inez returned to school after a week home in bed. She seemed about the same as before. Nickel had visited her every day after school and on weekends but, each time, he conveniently forgot to bring along the photograph she'd wanted to see — the one from the roof. Now that she was back on her feet, she insisted not only on seeing it, but on getting a real good look around the Beastly Arms. Nickel wasn't sure whether or not he should let her. He wasn't sure how Mr. Beastly would feel about it.

"But your parents won't let you go downtown," he said to her atop the monkey bars.

"That didn't stop us before!" Inez said. "Besides, Mama says I can go downtown so long as I'm not walking the streets down there alone or after dark."

"Why don't you wait until you're stronger?" Nickel said. He was grasping at straws.

Inez gave him a shove. "Stronger?" she said. "Watch this!" She dropped through the bars and walked, hand over hand, down the entire structure and back.

"Well, I can't today anyway," Nickel said. "I have to go to the college after school. Mom's expecting me. We have to do something."

"Something, huh?" Inez said, pulling herself back up. "All right. But count on it tomorrow." She pointed her finger at him. "Tomorrow!"

"Okay," Nickel said.

To Nickel's surprise, Mr. Beastly didn't object at all to letting Inez in on the secret.

"Who you trust, I trust," he said with a smile.

The next day Nickel and Inez took the 46 bus downtown. Inez said she was very impressed at how Nickel was able to find the alley all by himself. He knew she didn't mean it.

"New paint," she said of the door as Nickel slid in his key.

He took her to apartment 2D first, the barn owl's

room. When they opened the door, the owl twisted its head all the way around without turning its body. "Who!" it said.

Nickel had expected Inez to scream. But she didn't. He should have known better. He imagined nothing could scare Inez.

"You better keep Miriam out of here!" was all she said.

As Nickel took her from room to room, he retold the story Mr. Beastly had told him as best he could. Inez listened carefully and asked lots of questions. She loved the animals. The wood was her favorite part. She stretched her arms out wide and spun around and around.

"I think I'll be a forest ranger when I grow up!" she said.

"Not a marine biologist?" Nickel asked.

"Not today!" she said.

As time went on, Nickel helped out more and more with the maintenance of the Beastly Arms, giving Mr. Beastly more and more time for a long-deserved rest. Inez often came over after school and on weekends and pitched in. She took notes on all the animals in a spiral notebook. Nickel got his camera and the light meter his dad got him out of his drawer and shot pictures of the animals. He squeezed darkroom time in between school and his rounds at the Beastly Arms.

In the spring, he and Inez watched as the animals bore their young. The house was filled with higher-pitched sounds and a multitude of eggs. Inez wanted to name all the newborn.

"Name them and they're pets," Nickel said firmly. "These are wild animals. We don't own them. We're responsible for them. They own us."

"No one owns me," Inez said and started naming them anyway. She quit when Nickel showed her the spider eggs. There were thousands of them.

In June, Nickel and Inez graduated from the sixth grade. There was a ceremony in the school's auditorium. After much cajoling, Mr. Beastly put on his brown suit and tie and sat in the audience beside Nickel's mom, his brown felt hat in his lap. Nickel's dad was there, too, with Julie. They sat in a different row.

After the ceremony, at Mr. Beastly's suggestion, Nickel and his mom and Inez and her family and Mr. Beastly and Mr. Kirkaby all went downtown to an all-night deli. Nickel's dad didn't join them. He and Julie had a dinner date uptown. Before they left, though, Nickel's dad gave him his graduation present: an electric strobe.

"Your mom says you could use one," he said.

"Thanks," Nickel said, smiling. "I could."

The deli was called Mickey's. When the server came to their table, Mr. Beastly asked if Abe Micklenberg was still the owner, and the server went out back to get him.

"I can't believe it!" Mr. Micklenberg said when he saw Mr. Beastly. He was short and thin with gray whiskers, a large, bulbous nose and black eyes with deep, dark lines around them. Mr. Micklenberg was an otter — an otter with a blood-stained apron. "Julius Beasley!" he said. "I can't believe it! I heard you were dead!"

"People exaggerate," Mr. Beastly said with a grin. "I want you to meet my friends, Mickey. That's Mr. and Mrs. Willamina and their children, Inez and Cecil. And that's Mr. Kirkaby over there. He's a schoolteacher."

"Please to meet you, pleased to meet you," Mr. Micklenberg kept saying, nodding his head.

"And these are my dear friends, Maud Wilde and her son, Nicholas Dill. They live in my building. Nicholas has been a big help to me. He and Inez graduated sixth grade tonight."

"Well, congratulations!" Mr. Micklenberg said. He shook Nickel's hand. "You're a fine boy to help out an old man. You know, this Mr. Beasley made the building you're sitting in."

"I didn't build it, Mickey," Mr. Beastly said. "I just drew the pictures."

"Pictures, schmictures! He made it all right! Look, Julius, I'll bring some egg creams for the kids. Chocolate. I'll be right back." He walked away.

Inez stuck her tongue out. "What's an egg cream?"

"Chockit," Cecil said.

When Mr. Micklenberg returned, he had three foaming glasses on a tray. He gave Nickel, Inez, and Cecil each one, then proposed a toast. The adults lifted their water glasses. Nickel and Inez raised their egg creams. Cecil sucked on his straw.

"L'chaim!" Mr. Micklenberg said and clinked glasses with Mr. Beastly's.

"L'chaim!" Mr. Beastly said back. He clinked his glass with Nickel's mom and then everyone started clinking glasses.

"What did he say?" Inez whispered to Nickel.

Nickel shrugged.

"It means 'to life'!" Mr. Beastly said, his face red with happiness. "And I can't think of anything better to toast!"

Nickel's mom continued seeing Mr. Kirkaby over the summer, especially since they both had so much more free time. Mr. Kirkaby had no classes and Nickel's mom had given up waiting tables at Delphinium. The rent at the Beastly Arms was cheap enough she didn't have to. Ends were meeting.

Nickel didn't mind his mom dating Mr. Kirkaby now that Mr. Kirkaby wasn't his teacher anymore. He was just Duncan now, and besides, Nickel liked him. He always had, really. In fact, in August, when Nickel's mom suggested that they let Duncan in on the secret, Nickel had no objection at all. He even led him on the grand tour himself.

"Nickel," Duncan said, standing knee-deep in weeds in Sullivan Wood, "Mr. Beastly is a man who has made the most of his days."

After that, Duncan pitched in as well.

Despite his many protests, Nickel was still made to spend August in Oak Hollow with his dad. He hated being away from the Beastly Arms for so long. He whiled away the month playing with Miriam, talking to Inez on the phone, and visiting the public library, which was so far away that he had to be driven (there were no buses in Oak Hollow). He declined his dad's invitations to play golf on Sundays. Instead, he suggested they go camping in the country. His dad looked at him as if he were crazy.

"Never mind," Nickel said.

Then, finally, September came. School resumed. Even though their apartments were seventeen blocks apart, it turned out that Nickel and Inez lived in the same middle school district. The middle school was much bigger than their elementary school, with a lot more students, and, for the first time, Nickel and Inez had to change classes every fifty minutes. It was very confusing.

They had three classes together: English, algebra, and life science. In life science, they both stated on the first day that they would not be dissecting any animals under any circumstances, and then they each wrote notes for their parents to sign. Inez's went like this:

Dear Life Science Teacher,
Please excuse my daughter, Inez Willamina, from cutting open, slicing up, butchering, dismembering, maiming, or mutilating any living (or formerly living) creatures. Vivisection is against our religion.
Signed,

(Inez's mama)

23

ONE Saturday afternoon, Nickel stopped off at Mr. Beastly's room to hang a note on his door. (He never knocked on the door during the day. That was when Mr. Beastly slept.) The note read:

> Mr. B.—
> Everything okay. Plants all watered,
> see you tonight.
>
>   —N.

But then, as Nickel stood in the darkness attaching the note, the door opened. Mr. Beastly appeared in the doorway, backlit, his face in shadows. He was wearing his gray robe. His feet were bare.

"Come in a minute, son," he said in a gravelly voice.

Nickel stood there a moment, looking up at him. He had never been in Mr. Beastly's room.

"It's all right," Mr. Beastly said, waving him in. "I want to talk to you."

Nickel stepped slowly inside. He had always imagined that Mr. Beastly's room would have a dirt floor, like all the other rooms, and maybe even weeds and logs and bugs. But it didn't. The floor was made of cement and covered with a colorful woolen rug. It was the one that had been upstairs in the lobby, the one with the lion and the snake and the brightly colored bird with the flowing plumage — the quetzal. The rug was too large for the room, so it was rolled up at the edges. Miriam climbed down from Nickel's pocket and began nosing around for crumbs. A large furnace took up a lot of space in the corner, and made a constant rumbling noise. The rest of the room, minus a couch, an armchair, and a small table with an electric hot plate and a toaster on it, was given over to books. Bookshelves made of boards and bricks lined the walls, floor to ceiling. Every shelf was overflowing. Books were wedged in every which way. Nickel turned his head sideways, and scanned the spines. They were all about animals.

Nickel thought of all the bookshelves in his apartment — in 2E — and how there were none in any of the other rooms in the building. Then he remembered how the four-poster bed and the kitchen table had been left behind by a "former tenant," and, suddenly, he could see in his mind's eye the woolen rug spread out across the big floor in their living room. It wouldn't need to be rolled up, he thought. It would fit easily. Nickel had often wondered why Mr. Beastly had never converted 2E into a habitat. Now he knew.

"2E was your apartment, wasn't it?" he said.

Mr. Beastly smiled and shook his head in disbelief. "You're a remarkable young man, Nicholas Dill," he said.

"But you can't stay down here in the basement," Nickel said. "In this little room."

"I'm more than comfortable," Mr. Beastly said. "But thank you for your concern."

"You could move in with us. I'll sleep on the couch. I don't mind."

"No, Nicholas. This is my room now. I've taken root." His face turned serious. "And let's keep this to ourselves, okay, son? I know your mother would insist on a change, and it really isn't necessary. Things are perfect the way they are."

Nickel looked around at the room. It didn't seem perfect to him. But then he remembered how his mom had said that they should respect Mr. Beastly's privacy, so he promised not to say anything. He told himself, though, that he would look over the floor plans later and see if he could come up with a way of giving Mr. Beastly at least enough room to lay his rug out flat.

"Listen," Mr. Beastly said, "if there are any books you'd like to borrow, help yourself. There's no sense in them just sitting around gathering dust. Consider this the Beastly Arms Library!"

"The library!" Nickel said, standing up. "I'm supposed to meet Inez there at two!"

"Wait a second," Mr. Beastly said, putting his hand on Nickel's shoulder. "Sit down. I have something I want to talk to you about." Nickel could tell it was important. Mr. Beastly was acting like he did the night he told them about the Beastly Arms. Nickel sat down on the sofa. Miriam returned to his pocket with a plum pit she'd found. Mr. Beastly began pacing back and forth across the tiny room.

"I don't have anyone, you know," Mr. Beastly said. "No *people* anyway." He stopped and looked at Nickel for a second, then resumed his pacing. "And I'm not going to live forever," he went on. "Nothing does."

He stopped again. Nickel looked up at him with a confused expression, so Mr. Beastly sat down beside him.

"I've been waiting to discuss this with you for some time now." His eyes reddened around the edges. "You see, in the city, they need a caretaker." He looked deeply into Nickel's eyes. "The animals, I mean."

"The animals," Nickel repeated.

"Yes," Mr. Beastly said. "They need taking care of. And I can't do it forever."

Nickel looked at him carefully, at his wrinkled face and his tired eyes and his balding head, and for the first time he knew what kind of animal Mr. Beastly was. He was a human being. And now he also understood, for some reason, what Mr. Beastly was getting at.

"I'll be the caretaker," Nickel said. "I'll take care of all the animals." He smiled. "Including you."

"Oh, I can take care of myself!" Mr. Beastly said, taking a handkerchief from his robe pocket and blowing his nose in it. Miriam popped her head out of Nickel's pocket at the sound. Mr. Beastly smiled and added, "But I suppose I could use help from time to time."

Then suddenly, his expression shifted. He squinted at Nickel as if he'd seen something on his face he'd never noticed before.

"Has anyone ever told you you look just like a bush baby?"

Nickel beamed. "Just Inez," he said.

He jumped to his feet. A squeal of protest arose from his pocket. "I have to go!" he said, and rushed for the door. His camera, hanging from his neck on its strap, banged against his belly.

"Come back anytime!" Mr. Beastly called after him. "The Beastly Arms Library is always open! Well, nights mostly."

Nickel ran out into the hall, then stood still a moment in the dark, letting his eyes adjust. He saw Mr. Beastly's face in the darkness. He saw the barn owl, circling in the night sky. He saw Inez, doing cartwheels in the little patch of grass in front of the library.

And he ran off to meet her.

Nickel walked briskly the two miles or so up Ira Monk Street to the library that Mr. Beastly designed. The sky that day was filled with cumulus clouds — the best kind for animal-spotting — but Nickel kept his gaze at street level. He watched people going in and coming out of doors, stepping in and out of cars, climbing up into and down out of buses. He watched them walking their dogs and pushing strollers and just standing on street corners, talking. He saw them sitting or sleeping on the sidewalk. He watched the flocks of pigeons pecking at the pavement, walking along ledges, lifting off in waves. He smiled at the red and yellow leaves drifting down from the trees, and he heard them crunching under his feet. He remained aware of mailboxes and fire hydrants and safety cones and checked traffic before crossing the street. Miriam, no longer needed as a lookout, snoozed in his shirt pocket.

When Nickel passed the Gardenview Apartments, he slowed down a bit and gazed up at the window of his old room: third row of windows, second from the left. At the corner, he peered down 17th Street and saw Kleindienst's Bakery, Zindel's market, and Sixto on his corner, selling papers. It was too early for Agatha the pie lady.

At 18th Street, Nickel turned left. When he reached the library, Inez was out front, riding one of the concrete lions, pretending it was a bucking bronco.

"Howdy, pard!" she called out to Nickel. Her hair was unbraided. It billowed like a black cloud.

"Howdy," Nickel said. He took his light meter out of his pocket and metered, then brought his camera up to his eye and snapped Inez's picture.

They went in through the tall, bronze doors, through the vestibule, and past the circulation desk into the domed central hall. Here, Nickel stopped and gazed up at the dusty light shining in. His hands went up, cupped, trying to catch the motes in his hands. He began to spin slowly in place.

"Earth to Nickel," Inez whispered in his hear. "Earth to Nickel. Come in, please."

"I'm here," Nickel said. "Come on."

They went into the auditorium, where Ms. Blackburn had just finished her introduction. The lights went out and Nickel and Inez froze for a moment in the blackness. Then the projector came on and lit up the screen and they were able to see well enough to find two seats together.

"Just in time," Inez whispered as they sat down.

But Nickel didn't hear her. He was peeking into his pocket at Miriam, who saw this as a cue and hopped up his shirtfront. Nickel made a puckering sound and she tickled his lips with her whiskers. Then he raised his hand, closed in a fist, up to her mouth. Miriam sniffed at his knuckles. When he opened his fingers, there was a pumpkin seed in the center of his palm.